THE WEL
ET
D0735023

THE WELL AIN'T DRY YET

Belinda Anderson

Mountain State Press
Charleston, West Virginia

International Standard Book Number: 0-941092-43-7

Library of Congress Catalog Card Number: 2001-132158

First Edition
Printed in the United States of America

Monotype by Belinda Anderson
Cover design by Sharon Harms

Mountain State Press
2300 MacCorkle Avenue, S.E.
Charleston, WV 25304

This is a Mountain State Press book - Charleston, West Virginia. Mountain State Press is solely responsible for editorial decisions.

This is a work of fiction. Any references to historical events; to real people, living or dead; or to real locales are intended only to give the fiction a sense of reality and authenticity. Names, characters, places and incidents either are the product of the author's imagination or are used fictitiously, and their resemblance, if any, to real-life counterparts is entirely coincidental.

In memory of my father,
Leslie Anderson

Dedicated to my mother,
Ruth Anderson

Acknowledgments

First, thank you to Mountain State Press for promoting the voices of West Virginia authors. Special thanks go to eagle-eyed editor Carolyn Sturgeon.

Thank you to Lesley Toliver, one of the first readers of these stories, and to Gina Vitolo, Julie Weston and Anjali Banerjee, fellow writers who critiqued these pieces, providing excellent suggestions. Appreciation also goes to writers Karen Davis, Ann Penn and Brad Stansberry, who supported my early efforts.

Thank you to Barbara Smith, Cathy Pleska, George Lies and the other folks involved with encouraging writers through West Virginia Writers, Inc.

I also want to thank my English teachers, who had a profound influence in my life. Because of Mrs. Geiger, I began a journal in seventh grade. In high school, Mrs. Miller and Mrs. Muncy encouraged me to pursue my writing dreams. Thank you to my writing students, who continually freshen my own enthusiasm with their blossoming creativity.

Family is an important theme in this collection and in my own life. I'm blessed to have my mother, Patricia, Jimmy, David, Lesley, Paul, Andrew, Dwayne, Arlene, Anthony and Heather.

Thank you to my family and friends for support and encouragement. I appreciate each of you.

And, finally, thanks to the characters who visit and share their secrets.

Contents

Twilight Dawn

I was made from star light, my grandmother told me. She took me to raise after my momma died. My grandmother was born a slave on a piddling tobacco farm in Virginia, but she was the proudest woman I ever knew. She told me I was somebody. "You got divine light in you, child," she would say, taking hold of my chin and staring straight into my eyes for so long that I felt the universe start to swell inside me. I still hold the universe, even though my joints crack and my hair looks like bleached steel wool.

My name is Twilight Dawn Johnson. I am an old, old woman, but I got a pile of work to do before I can go. There's a lot more folks need my quilts before I can lay down my needle and thimble.

It don't seem like my sight is as good as it used to be, and I know my mind wanders like a cow in the woods, but somehow my stitches turn out just as small and even as ever. My hands seem to move now without my guidance, the silver needle winking in and out of the cloth, stitching one little ridge after another.

If I thought my eyes were bad before, this quilt will blind me. Some fellow brought over enough bolts of fabric to make a rainbow. I'm talking scalding red, yellow, orange, blue and green. "It's for a special friend of ours, a young woman who hasn't had it very easy," he said. "Mother asked me to see if you could make a starburst pattern." I examined his kindly face and I knew he'd adopt every orphan in the world if he could. I also knew right away that I'd make a Star Everlasting quilt.

Orphaned is just what one blonde-haired woman was feeling when she stood in my living room clutching her daddy's beach shirts. She said she wanted me to piece a quilt from those clothes, but I could tell she wanted to run when she spotted the scissors lying beside my cardboard diamond pattern.

"They say you do wonderful work," she said, ready to cry.

I took the shirts from her. "Honey, I'm going to make you a happy memory quilt. You just leave all this with me." I already knew I'd make her a Trip Around the World, even though cutting and sewing all those little bitty squares is hard on my eyes.

People seem happy with what I give them. Well, I had one complaint about price from Wanda -- hmm, right now I can't recall her last name. All I said was, "That's what it's worth to me to do the work. If you want to find somebody else, that's fine." I quit arguing with people a long time ago. I've never seen an argument yet that changed anybody's mind.

"Well, I'm already here," she said, and handed me a Wal-Mart bag filled with small triangles her grandmother had cut from feed sacks, but never got around to quilting. Wanda wanted me to make a quilt for her cousin Dotty.

"If I was you, I might be tempted to keep this for myself," I told her. "There's history here."

"Dotty never had much growing up," she said. "Besides, I've held on to these old scraps too long." Then I knew her for a woman who was generous, despite her vinegary words. I sewed those triangles into diamonds and made a Lemon Star quilt.

And so they keep coming to me, from Lewisburg, Bluefield, Princeton, even out of state. I don't go anywhere. I've lived on this border all my life. It's always made me a little uneasy, roosting where West Virginia parts company with Virginia. I am one hundred percent West Virginian and proud of it. But there's a lot of West Virginia I don't know anything about. Never been to a coal camp. Never even toured the exhibition coal mine in Beckley. I hear there are glass factories all over the state, but I couldn't tell you a thing about them.

My piece of West Virginia looks more the way my grandmother described the Shenandoah Valley of the Old Dominion. Monroe County is an earthen quilt of green farmland patches, stitched in place by chains of mountains. My trailer roosts in a valley, so I can quilt in my living room and look out the window at those beautiful hunks of blue and green.

My land may resemble parts of Virginia, but those folks don't seem like my people. When my grand-niece left her husband and went to work in Roanoke, people at work teased her, called her a hillbilly, told terrible jokes about incest. I believe they're still smarting over losing a big chunk of land during the War Between the States, so they try to make themselves look bigger at the expense of others. They keep gnawing that old bone. Of course, this part of West Virginia was mostly sympathetic to the Confederates. I've heard politicians used the war and the issue of slavery as an excuse to grab power from Richmond. All I know for sure is what my grandmother taught me, never to take freedom for granted.

My grandmother taught me the secret of the Underground Railroad when she taught me to quilt. Slaves couldn't read, but they could creep up to a yard and see a cotton quilt hanging on a clothesline. Certain quilts spelled freedom. Birds in the Air, that was safe. And Tail of Benjamin's Kite. The Evening Star pattern gave directions.

Most folks today hem themselves in. Take my grand-niece's ex-husband, for example. Randall is all right for a white boy -- who knows what that girl was thinking when she took up with him -- but he doesn't have a lick of gumption. He's just waiting on life to happen. His cousin, Jason, doesn't have any gumption, either. He wastes his life drinking beer and chasing women, just because he thinks he was cheated out of his chance at the Big Leagues. He's still grieving over what might have been. And don't even get me started on that other cousin that headed south to find himself, leaving his wife to raise their boy alone. I worry about the boy. He's got a dark, inky shadow in his heart.

I worry just as much about that Serena. Her mother brought her by when she came to pick up a quilt. That young woman has the attention span of a chicken and a tongue that loves to flap. She went on and on about how she's going to become a famous writer, just like Louisa May Alcott. That girl doesn't know enough to doubt herself. I fear she'll get bruised in this old world.

It would be hard to raise a child like that, trying to make her understand without ruining her spirit. I never had children. Never married. Never been away from these hills. Got my heart broke once and decided to keep the pieces to myself. I learned a lot about life, anyway. People bring their stories to me, telling me more with their bits of fabric than they ever could with words. A girl gently unfolds a tattered old gown, running her fingers over the rough lace before she hands it to me. A widower brings me a dozen silk scarves, as bright and fine as the woman who wore them.

"Jimmy! Edward Thurman Junior!" Sounds like I've got company. By the time I get to the screen door, two moon-faced rascals, one with red hair and one with yellow, have beheaded half a dozen of my tulips. "Quit it, y'all," hollers a good-sized woman unloading herself from a minivan. They pay her no mind whatsoever until she says, "I reckon you don't want to go to the Cracker Barrel, after all." The boys leave the flowers and start chasing each other around the yard.

"I'm sorry, hi, I'm Margaret." For such a big voice, it holds a lot of doubt. "Are you--um, the quilter?"

"That's me, honey. Come on in." I hold the screen door open for her.

"Oh, no, I don't have time." She's carrying a plastic bag. She starts to give it to me, then stops. "Could you make a quilt from the boys' baby clothes?"

She wants something to hold and remember the sweet clean smell of her newborns. When the boys are at school and her husband's at work, she'll wrap herself in that quilt and think back to the time when sticky, chubby little hands used to wind around her neck.

The woman whips her head at a big cracking noise, the sound of wood screaming. "Jimmy! Junior!" And then I see them. Those boys have ruined my grape trellis trying to play Tarzan. They're standing there, looking mighty disappointed at the vine lying torn and shredded on the ground, the vine my grandmother brought from Virginia. "That's it -- you can forget about the Cracker Barrel."

The boys start howling. "You promised," the redhead says.

"You said we could order breakfast for supper." The blond one wipes his nose with the back of his hand.

"I said we'd stop if you behaved yourselves." Margaret turns to me. "I'm really sorry. Can I pay you for that?"

How could she ever replace the one living, breathing tie to the woman who showed me my soul? I feel my blood heating and percolating through my thready old veins. Well. There's a surprise. I thought I was done with anger. Anger don't do a thing but eat at the spirit, unless you can do some good with it, like Dr. King.

"You must think I'm a terrible mother." Those eyes are the palest blue, but I can't see any light in them.

"I'll make your quilt," I say, reaching for the bag. I'm going to piece Grandmother's Flower Garden. I'll cut those powdery pale baby clothes into real delicate-looking blossoms. She needs something soft and pretty.

"We've caused you enough trouble," she says.

"Honey," I tell her. "Let go of the bag." And all of a sudden, she does. She starts like a deer that just heard the first blast of hunting season, grabs hold of her children and drives off. I walk over to the trellis, but I'm too stiff to bend down and pick up the vine. I wish I could hold it just one time before it withers.

Letting go is the hardest thing. I was just seventeen when I found my grandmother slumped over a Log Cabin quilt she had just finished. When I lifted her cheek from the cloth, I looked more closely at the pattern. Instead of using red patches in the centers of the squares, she had sewn the dark blue signal of freedom.

I didn't see how I could live without her. They found me rocking her in my arms, petting her hair, singing her favorite hymns. It took me a long, long time to learn that holding on hurts worse than letting go.

I look at that old vine again. It will return to the earth. The earth is part of the universe that lives in me, and my grandmother's spirit rides the Milky Way.

I go back in the house and settle down at the quilt frame again. I need to finish this Star Everlasting. Got a lot of work to get done before my century is completed. People need these quilts. With every pull on the thread, I try to stitch them a little hope.

Reunion

If only I had thrown out that invitation to that 20th-year class reunion. Now I can't seem to find the right excuse. "I can't dance." I grew up in a church that claimed you could go to hell for such shenanigans. Of course, I don't believe that hogwash anymore, but I still can't dance.

"No problem," Ed says. This is his mantra. "No problem whatsoever. We'll go to the banquet and then cut out. Besides, I mostly want to go to the afternoon social."

"And just what kind of social can you have in the parking lot of a doughnut shop?"

Ed proceeds to tell me about joyful evenings hanging around in muscle cars, smoking and jawing. And the ritual of being rousted by the town cop. Then he explains how he's planning to blow into town, roaring through town in his arrest-me-red Corvette.

"And what good-looking woman are you planning on getting to go with the Vette?" I ask.

"You, of course."

"You know I can't handle that car." Now, a Corvette is a smooth-looking car. I'll give you that. It runs like a scalded dog. But you can't get in and out of the damned thing because it squats so low to the ground. I mean, you basically have to fall into it to sit down. Then you're crammed in there, loaded up like some Olympic athlete headed down one of those ice chutes. Exiting is a real trick. Especially when you've had a couple of kids and carry a few pounds over fighting weight. I tried riding in the car once and immediately demanded to be returned to my minivan. I can just see myself tumbling out of the Vette, rolling and rolling until I wind up at the feet of his laughing classmates.

Ed just stands there, smiling at me like Howdy Doody. Ed doesn't worry about what people think. That's evident from his haircut. Apparently it amuses the barber to trim Ed's copper thatch so his big ears can flap freely. You couldn't guess by looking at him that he's a top-earning salesman. But he moves NASCAR memorabilia like nobody's business. I believe he could sell coolers to Eskimos. People just love him. He knows how to make them feel good. Retailers call him if they haven't seen him for a couple of weeks. They suggest increasing their order.

I love him, too. But if he thinks I'm getting in that car, he's got another think coming.

Ed takes my hand. "Come on, Margaret."

I stand my ground, immovable as Lot's wife. I'm a harder sell. I'm determined to ignore those big blue eyes with the laugh crinkles. Now he cocks his head like a puzzled pup. "For me, sugarpie?"

I am defeated. "All right," I sigh. Ed beams and leads me to the garage. "The first time is the worst. You just need to get adjusted to the Vette. Here, just try sitting in it for a little bit." He opens the door to the beast. I turn my back to the passenger seat, grab on to his arm and begin to lower myself.

"Atta girl," he praises, pulling back his arm.

All right, that wasn't so bad. But now I'm at eye level with my feet. I try to lift my left leg, but I can't get any momentum. Finally, I grab my left leg under the knee and drag the limb inside. Then the right. OK. I'm in.

"There, that wasn't so bad, was it?" Ed has to squat to talk to me face to face.

My lower back already hurts. "Let me out of here." Ed stands and offers his hand, but I'm not sure how to go about raising the Titanic. "Hold on. Let me think about this." I decide to simply reverse the process. I fling my legs over the door sill and turn to face the opening. Ed extends both hands and I grab on. He starts tugging at me, and I try to push up.

Just then I hear a holler and a yelp. Startled, I let go and drop back inside the Vette. Jimmy comes running into the garage, his brother right on his heels. "Mommy, Junior hit me."

Junior turns to his dad. "Jimmy started it--"

"Edward Thurman Junior, you know better than to hit your brother," I say. "Now, both of you quit it." It might be worth going to the reunion just to dump these two with their grandmother for a couple of nights.

"But--" Junior starts.

"You boys heard your mother." Instantly, they cease and desist. Fluffy strolls over to the scene and parks, narrowing her gaze at me in that superior attitude that cats reserve for the simple beings that exist to fill their food bowls. Then she begins grooming her white fur.

Jimmy eyeballs me with interest. "Whatcha doing?"

"Nothing you need to worry about." It's a hot day, and I'm starting to sweat and stick to the black leather. But I can reach out and brush back the hair obscuring his blue eyes. My hair used to be that pretty corn yellow. "Go on with your brother."

But now Junior is standing in front of me, a miniature version of his father. "You can't get out, can you?"

He may look like his dad, but somewhere he picked up a smart mouth. "Yes, I can get out. Now, go on and play."

Instead, the rascal turns to Jimmy. "I bet you a quarter she can't get out. They'll have to get the rescue squad to haul her out of there."

Jimmy bursts into tears. "Mommy, are you going to die?" He knows his Paw-paw never returned after the paramedics took him to the hospital.

Finally, Ed grinds into action. "Now, boys, there's nothing wrong. Me and your mom are just horsing around."

"Yeah, right," Junior says.

"Ed, if you don't get them out of here right now--" I feel a mustache of perspiration trembling over my mouth.

"Come on, fellas." Ed herds them outside.

"Now help me out of here." Ed grabs my hands and begins pulling again. He's working up a sweat, too. The bucket seat sucks at me like a Hoover. But I keep grunting and pushing, while Ed pulls at me like he's hauling in a snapping turtle on his fishing line.

Suddenly, I shoot out of there and straight into Ed's arms, nearly knocking him down. Ed straightens up and gives me a squeeze. "Whoa, honeybun. There's time for that later." He winks at me and gives me a kiss before I can light into him. The touch of his lips still sends a sizzle down my spine. I can't seem to recall the biting remark I was about to deliver.

Well, I guess we're going. Somehow, I find myself packing a suitcase. I guess it won't be such a bad ride from Hinton to Huntington. I hear a god-awful yowl and I rush to the back porch. Junior clutches Fluffy's back legs, while Jimmy has hold of the other end. They're swinging the poor, crying cat back and forth and Junior is counting, "One, two--"

"Put that cat down right now!" I holler.

That surprises them enough to drop her. Fluffy scampers away. "I wish you all would quit torturing that cat."

"Aw, we wasn't going to hurt her," Junior informs me. "We're conducting an experiment." Jimmy nods to back up his brother.

"Go on."

"We wanted to see if cats really land on their feet." Jimmy nods again.

"So you were just going to give her a pitch?"

"Exactly."

I'm about to light into him when Fluffy saunters back to the porch. She begins winding herself around first Jimmy and then Junior, purring and rubbing like they're all best buddies. "See how she trusts you? You need to be more careful with her." I turn back to the house. Poor dumb animal. Doesn't have enough sense to stay out of harm's way.

"Hoo, hoo, hoooo." Ed is singing like a rock-and-roll owl to an old Steve Miller Band song and the Corvette is lapping up the interstate. He's feeling good. Real good. If I hear one more greatest hit, I'm going to scream.

We're nearing Huntington when Ed starts closing in on a dark green Jag. He stops singing. "Looky there," he said. "XJ12." Ed moves into the passing lane, but he doesn't pass. Instead, he pulls up beside the Jag and waves at the driver.

"Ed, what do you think you're doing?"

Ed just grins. His brain already has leapt back to high school. He wants to race. I sneak a look to my right.

The driver is a distinguished-looking older gentleman, with longish white hair and a neat, dark suit. He catches my eye and smiles at me, kindly. I turn away, embarrassed. "For God's sake, Ed, quit fooling around. You'll get us killed."

"Aw, I'm just--" Suddenly he swerves back to the right lane and dives onto a ramp. "Oops, just about missed the exit. Wouldn't have been much of a match, anyway. Bet that thing leaks oil bad." Ed roars through Huntington just as he had threatened, brakes hard and turns into the doughnut shop parking lot, spewing gravel.

People stand around, making awkward stabs at conversation. All heads swivel at the sight and sound of Ed's Vette. If his grin stretches any further, it'll pin those big ears to his head. The crowd begins to close in on the Vette. I look up at the open mouths and vacant eyes of the alum trying to identify us. "Night of the Living Dead," I mutter.

"What's that, honeybun?" Ed doesn't even draw breath to let me answer. "You sit tight. I'll help you out." He leaps out of the Vette like a jackrabbit. As soon as his old classmates see those ears, they yell, "Jughead!" The guys slap him on the back and make admiring remarks about his car. The women hug him close. I sit there like a beta in a bowl until someone peers through the windshield. "Who you got in there, Eddie?"

"What's that?" Then I see his head snap around as he remembers that there's a wife wedged in his dream machine. Ed rushes over to the passenger door. He opens it and extends his hand. I smile at the faces looming over me. Well, it's now or never. I begin my new exit technique. I swing my legs out and bend forward, one hand resting against the seat bolster. The push-off is the key to success. I call up every ounce of strength I have to propel myself. I reach out with my other hand to grab Ed's.

I hear the grumbling menace of another sports car entering the parking lot. Out of the corner of my eye, I see a black Porsche 911. The men whistle. "Wow," one woman says. "Now, that's sweet," one of the guys adds. Ed whips his head around to check out the challenger. Unfortunately for me, his body follows his noggin's lead. My hand meets empty air. Too bad the rest of me already launched. I pitch forward from my half-hunched position and hit the asphalt. I roll a couple of times, coming to rest on my back, looking up at a circle of wide-eyed faces. The horror.

We all seem to float in silence for a few moments. Then Ed is propping me up. "Sugarpie, you OK?"

"I think so." Except for the total humiliation.

The Porsche opens and the driver strides toward me, his blonde-haired companion trotting beside him. He removes his aviator sunglasses and gives me one of Fluffy's appraising glances. "Let me make sure you didn't break anything before you try to stand." He presses around here and there. After he's satisfied that I'm in one piece, he and Ed help me to my feet. I brush gravel from my outfit. Then I stare for awhile at the palms of my hands, dented with the imprints of stone. You know how they always say nothing can be as bad as you imagine? Well, that's another one of those damn lies.

I blow out a big breath and work up the nerve to look at the bunch of Baby Boomers surrounding me. They're absolutely silent, like a mob in a Western waiting for the stranger to say the wrong thing so they can hang him. "Well," I hear myself saying. "How's that for an entrance?" The crowd laughs, Ed beams and the moment passes.

I don't really care for alcohol. That was something else that could send you straight to hell, according to the church. When I finally sampled a drink, I found I didn't care for the bitter taste. But after five minutes of milling aimlessly around the country club banquet room, I make a beeline for the bar, leaving Ed to tell a group of guys more of his up-close-and-personal stories of race car drivers. "What can I get for you?" asks the polite young man.

"I don't know. Something kind of light."

"Maybe a white zinfandel?" He reaches for a wine glass.

"No, no, I'm allergic to sulfites." Bloating is the last thing I need right now. "Do you have something with a sweet taste?"

The bartender brightens. "Here you go." He pours me a little glass of liqueur. "Peach schnapps."

I brighten, too. They drank schnapps in the early days of *Mission: Impossible*. The team could always count on Barbara Bain and a bottle of schnapps to distract the East Bloc enemy. I take a cautious sip. Mmmm. I like that nice warmth sliding down my throat. I take another sip. I gaze around coolly, with the same slight smile that Cinnamon employed to assess dire situations.

The women and men just don't seem to match. Most of the men look a little worn by life -- some balding, some paunching, coughing as they smoke nervously. The women look suspiciously good. Tight abs, smooth faces, nary a strand of gray. I feel ugly, overweight and out of place. I'm no Cinnamon. One of the divine creatures floats my way. It's the blonde from the Porsche. She's wearing a gorgeous black dress that highlights her tan and golden hair. She drifts to the bar and procures a club soda.

She squints at my name tag that identifies me as a spouse. "Margaret, that's a pretty name. I'm Diane. Navy is a really good color for you. You're Eddie's wife? Do you have children?" Somehow, she can smile and talk at the same time.

"Yes, we've got two boys."

"That's wonderful. We've got two girls and two boys. My husband's a surgeon." I was prepared to resent her childless figure, but now I have to hate her. She takes the barest sip from her club soda. "I'm almost afraid to drink anything. I'm afraid I'll bust right out of this dress." She lowers her voice to conspirator level. "I started dieting the moment I heard they were organizing this." She speaks quickly, urgently, as though she's running out of time. "Started hitting the tanning salon, too. And I could swim in all the cream I've smeared on my face."

Why is she telling me all this? "Well, you look terrific," I say.

Diane shakes her head in dismissal of the compliment. "I just wanted to look decent. You know? I got picked on so much in school. Why are people so mean? Do you know my best friend wouldn't even come? Just because she's always been, well, full-figured. I told her to come here and show them what a success she has become. I mean, she's got a doctorate and she works at some think tank in Washington. You want to talk local girl makes good? But she said nobody would be interested in her life, just in seeing if she put on any more weight."

She seems oblivious to the fact that this might make me feel even more self-conscious. Then she says, "I wish I could be more like you." I find this hard to believe, but she keeps talking. "I would have died of embarrassment if I had fallen out of a car like that. I would have just tucked my tail and gone back home, crying all the way." And that's exactly what I would have done if I could have operated the Corvette's manual transmission. "But you just dusted your hands and made some funny comment like it was no big deal. And it wasn't. You just handled the situation so well."

I stare at her, stunned. "But--" I'm cut off by Diane's husband.

"What are you drinking?" He sounds angry.

"It's just club soda--"

"Excuse us," the man says to me, then grabs her elbow and steers her away.

"You having a good time, honeybun?" Ed is a happy camper, filled with roast beef and peach cobbler. I nod, noticing that my head feels heavier than usual. The awards for most gray hair and least changed have been doled out. And now the DJ takes over, cranking up the music to an ear-crushing volume.

The DJ begs people to get up and dance, but everyone seems to be holding back and waiting for someone else to begin. Just like high school. "Don't reckon I could persuade you to dance with me?" Ed tries the pup pose, but I shake my head.

And then ABBA bursts from the speakers. I love those Swedes. They can transform anything into melodrama. I start tapping my foot in time to the beat of "Dancing Queen."

And then I see Diane glide onto the floor by herself. At first, she stands in place, eyes closed, moving her body ever so slightly like a caterpillar trying to decide if it's ready to become a butterfly. All conversation stops. The entire room is gaping at Diane. Then she stretches her arms as though she's ready to try her wings. She opens her eyes, but I don't think she sees us. Her graceful movements grow larger. She begins to spin with the music. She whirls faster and faster as the sweet voices of Agnetha and Frida warble for this dancing queen. Sweat begins to shine on her face.

Suddenly, her husband rushes onto the dance floor. He grabs her arm. "You're making a fool of yourself. I knew you were drinking."

The music keeps blaring, but Diane stops. I can tell from her face that she's about to burst into tears. I grab Ed's hand. "Come on, we've got to do something." And bless that man, he doesn't even question me.

I walk over to the DJ and place my order. The twang of country rock chords bursts from the speakers and Steve begins a jovial refrain about his dancing and singing grandparents, begging his own girl to join in. "Dance, dance, dance," he carols.

"Come on, everybody," Ed shouts. "Diane got us started. Let's cut the rug." And Ed and I start dancing like the middle-aged fools that we are. I don't care if I look smooth or cool. I just bob my head and rotate my hips and hope for the best. The person who should be embarrassed loosens his grip on Diane. Other couples drift toward us and start to sway to the music. Diane's face smoothes and she smiles. I smile, too.

"Dance, dance, dance," Steve urges us. My husband takes me in his arms.

Rainbow Ranch

My neighbor dips his brush in a can and applies another stroke of startling baby blue. He's painting the river rocks lining his driveway. Then he pauses, like he knows someone's watching him. He stretches his old, long frame and raises his hand as if to wave toward my window. Quickly, I release the edge of the curtain and walk away.

When I moved in three days ago, he was just trimming the white frame house. His selection of color was a little sugary for my taste, but I figured I should be glad he kept his property maintained. Then the old fellow got carried away. He dabbed bright blue paint on the post supporting the mailbox with a laughing fox drawn on the side. Then, the chimney. Next, three tractor tires, coated powder blue, appeared in the front yard. He planted petunias in them at the direction of his wife. I guess she's his wife. They look like a matched set, anyway -- lean, and white-haired.

Bright splashes of color make me uncomfortable. I try to avoid attracting attention. My wardrobe consists of varying shades of brown and my hair stays trimmed at my shoulders -- not too short, not too long. Someone once called my hair honey, but it's not really anything, not definitively light or dark. The manufacturer named the paint of my compact car, "Silver Thunder," but it's really gray. I rented this little stucco house because it's plain, but neat, squeezed between a small brick ranch and the dwelling that's now decorated like a cupcake. At my new job, I sit in a little cubicle where I don't even have to talk to people face to face. The callers just give me their order information and I type it on my keyboard.

The doorbell rings. I stand very still, trying not to even breathe too loudly, hoping whoever it is will go away. It rings a second time. A woman's voice tentatively calls, "Hello?" Then she says, "Maybe we've come at a bad time. Let's just leave it here."

I wait until dark to crack open the door. It's a basket of food. I feel ashamed. Those old folks are just trying to be nice to me. Carrying the basket to the kitchen table, I unload bright flowered cloth napkins, a loaf of banana bread and a small jar neatly labeled, "Blackberry jam, Myra Fox."

Saturday morning, I tell myself I'm a grown woman, and I follow the pastel trail to my neighbors' house. But when I get there, I decide to just drop the empty basket on the porch. Before I can flee, Mr. Fox opens the door. "Look, Mother! It's our new neighbor."

Mrs. Fox appears at her husband's side and takes his arm. "How nice!"

I thrust the basket at them. "Um, I just wanted to thank you and make sure I returned your--"

"Isn't that nice?" Mrs. Fox asks her husband. "Very thoughtful. I can tell you're that kind of person."

"Well, come right in," Mr. Fox says, holding the door wide open.

"Oh, really, I can't--" I start backing up, but Mrs. Fox lays a hand on my arm.

"Please." I stare at the hand on my arm, wondering if she feels the nervous perspiration. Then I look into her face, into the most incredibly compelling eyes, beautiful swirls of blue and green. "I just made peach cobbler. Why, I don't know. Both of us are supposed to watch our sugar."

I find myself drawn into a vortex of yellow. The dark-gold appliances from some long-ago decade look positively subtle compared to the rest of the room. The linoleum twinkles with speckles of amber and topaz. A wallpaper border of daffodils tops the pale lemon walls. More flowers pattern the curtains, dish towels and pot holders.

Somehow, I'm sitting at an oak table, nervously forking peach cobbler in my mouth. My sated taste buds loosen my tongue a little. "This is delicious." Mrs. Fox glows at me.

"Have some more. You young people burn off calories so fast." Before I know it, I've told the Foxes that my name is Andrea, I'm 28, single and a recent transplant from Blacksburg returning to my native West Virginia. A glass of skim milk later, I know that the Foxes have a daughter teaching school in Montana and that the couple worked for years as supervisors at a facility for abused and neglected children.

"I wish our girl would come home," Mrs. Fox says. "What brought you back?"

I focus on the empty glass for awhile. "A better job, for one thing. But mostly, the mountains." I don't know how to begin explaining how safe I feel nestled among the softly forested mountains. Or how exposed I felt away from them. But the Foxes smile at me like they know exactly what I mean.

"Would you like to see the rest of the house?" Mr. Fox asks.

"Well--" I don't even know these people.

"Please." Mrs. Fox's jewel-bright eyes capture me and next thing I know I'm traipsing through the house of strangers, following the couple down the hallway. Mrs. Fox walks stiffly, taking her husband's arm for support. First stop on the tour, the bathroom. Suddenly, I'm in an aquarium that just happens to be equipped with a toilet and an old claw-footed tub. Happy dolphins swim on azure-washed walls. Small, blueberry-colored soaps shaped like starfish rest in a glass shell on the sink. The toilet lid and tank top snuggle under fuzzy sapphire covers.

"We never got to the ocean, so we made our own island paradise," Mr. Fox says and laughs.

"Here's our room," Mrs. Fox says as her husband opens a door. Green. Nothing but green. Jade carpeting. Ivy trailing down wallpaper colored as pale as a peeled cucumber. A smaller pattern of ivy decorating a bedspread and draperies colored as lightly as just-formed apples. "It's very soothing, don't you think?"

Numbly, I nod my head and follow them along the hallway again, turning into the living room. Pink pours from the tiny room -- rosy pearl carpet, matching mauve sofa and chairs, blushing wallpaper covered with roses.

"Sit, sit." Mr. Fox gestures to a pink chair. "Mother, you too. You've been on your feet all morning." The Foxes sit side by side on the pink sofa and smile contentedly at me. Mr. Fox tucks a little pillow behind his wife's back.

"Well," Mrs. Fox says. I nod and pluck at my beige pants.

"Well," Mr. Fox says. I nod again. "So what do you think of our rainbow ranch?"

"It's very--" I swallow. "Very distinctive."

Mrs. Fox laughs. "He came home from the hardware store one day with all these cans of paint. When I asked him what in the world he was celebrating, all he said was, 'I'm going to paint this place in all your favorite colors.' When I asked him why on earth for, do you know what he said?"

I shake my head.

" 'Because I love you.' That was the only answer I ever got out of him." She pats his hand. "I believe he might be the sweetest man on this earth."

I blink back tears. The love radiating from these two pulses through the room like a living entity.

Mr. Fox coughs in embarrassment, then smiles. "Of course, I didn't realize Mother was going to take a fresh coat of paint as a cue to drain the bank account."

Mrs. Fox winks at me. "I don't think redecorating once every twenty or thirty years is unreasonable, do you?"

"No, ma'am," I agree.

"Do you think the exterior is too much?" Mr. Fox asks.

"Well--"

"I thought I'd grab a dab of heaven." Mr. Fox stretches his arms toward the window. "Sky to earth." Sun trickles through the window, highlighting the room until I begin to feel a little rosy myself. I think I like these strange neighbors.

My other neighbor, Mr. Wood, is a short, cranky old buzzard who likes to brag about how many pounds he can still bench press. He probably could crack my neck like a chicken bone.

The day I first met him, we happened to be checking our mailboxes at the same time. As I was working up my nerve to make some neighborly comment, he frowned at me and said, "You plan on mowing your yard some time in the near future? You wait much longer, you'll have to call the road crew from the highway department." I just stood there with my mouth open as he walked back to his house.

It's a week later, and I'm still trying to think of a smart comeback. I know I wouldn't say it, but I wish I could think up one, anyway. Like, "How about loaning me your mower?" I never had a house before. I had no idea lawn equipment was so expensive. Lucky for me, Mr. Fox just showed up one day and offered me the use of his mower. Actually, he volunteered to cut the grass for me, but I couldn't accept.

Mr. Wood marches to his plain metal mailbox, then over to my lot just as I'm about to start the mower. "Damn circus," he says.

"Excuse me?"

He points down the street. "That. Disgrace to the neighborhood." I think it was the addition of the blue birdbath that finally got him.

"It is different," I say, trying to be as neutral as possible.

Mr. Wood steps toward me. Too close. "I tell you what--" I don't hear the rest. I crank the mower to a roar and turn away. I don't like people getting in my face, or too near, period.

The mower quits on me. I check the gas. Plenty in the tank. Probably got a chunk of still-wet grass in the blade. Suddenly, I whirl around, nearly knocking the mower over at the touch of a hand to my shoulder.

"I'm sorry, Andrea," Mr. Fox says. "I didn't mean to startle you. I was just wondering if you wanted to borrow my clippers to trim around the trees." His hand rests on my shoulder. I try not to jerk away, but I can't stop myself from stiffening involuntarily, and he gently drops his hand.

Several days pass and Mr. Fox remains as friendly as ever, but he is careful not to touch me. I feel more comfortable, yet sometimes I yearn for the warmth of that fatherly clasp. Today, he's helping me paint my kitchen. I decided maybe my own place could use a little perking up, so Mr. Fox accompanied me to the hardware store. He pounced on the tropical tangerine, but I wanted to buy the creamy beige. We finally compromised on pale apricot. It's amazing how even this small hint of color warms the room.

"It sure is nice of you to help me," I tell Mr. Fox as I roll another stripe of apricot on the last wall.

"It's my pleasure. Oh, Mother wanted me to invite you to supper. She's fixing baked chicken and mashed potatoes."

"I don't know. I appreciate it, but I've got a lot to do." I'd love to eat supper every evening with the Foxes in their blazing house, but I feel like I ought to keep a little distance.

"I expect you've got better things to do than to hang out with a couple of antiques." Mr. Fox neatly brushes around the woodwork. "But Mother sure does brighten up when you visit."

"Me?"

"She's always loved being around people, but that damned arthritis keeps her at home most of the time. She doesn't complain, but I know she's in pain." Mr. Fox dips his brush in the paint can. "She says you're a breath of fresh air."

The next day, I show up at the door with a small bag in my hand. Mrs. Fox answers my knock. "Andrea! What's that you've got there? A gift for me, I hope. Lucky that Father's down at the hardware store. I won't have to share." I grin back at her. I can't resist these people.

"It's a box of tea. Green tea. It's supposed to be very healthy for you."

"Isn't that nice?" Mrs. Fox leads me into the kitchen. "Let's have some." It is nice being in this kitchen again. Even on a summer day, the golden glow is welcome. We sit at the oak table, sipping tea. I notice how carefully she concentrates on pouring, that she winces as she sets the heavy pot on the table. Then she smiles at me. "You look gorgeous in that color. Makes your hair shine and your eyes sparkle like chocolate drops."

I look down at the saffron top that I just bought on impulse. "I don't know. I just never thought about wearing this color."

"I believe you might surprise and delight yourself, given half a chance." I run my fingers along the rim of the tea cup, blooming with yellow roses. I can't answer her.

"Andrea." I look up and am immediately caught by those glowing aquamarine eyes. Mrs. Fox leans across the table and takes my hands. "I just want to tell you how much I appreciate your friendship." I take a deep breath, willing myself not to jerk away from the contact. I hadn't noticed before the frailty of her own flesh. She cocks her head sideways and draws back. "I'm sorry. I don't mean to embarrass you."

Her smile fades to a sorrowful expression, but she continues to focus on me with so much kindness and love in her eyes. I can't bear it. Then, suddenly, something inside me -- something that's been closed off for a long time -- cracks wide open. Sunshine floods the kitchen and seems to bounce off the bright walls and straight into that new fissure in my heart. It feels strange, this new warmth.

I find myself reaching out, clasping her hands in mine. Her smile returns, brighter than before. "Andrea," she says, "You're going to be all right."

I slept so well last night that I'm up early enough to treat the Foxes to breakfast before I head to work. I dress quickly, swipe the toothbrush back and forth a couple of times and hurry next door.

I can't believe it. The mailbox rests in the yard, beside the broken post. The petunias, yanked from the tires, lie with their stems broken like smashed vertebrae. Mr. Fox is staring at a pile of blue rubble that used to be the birdbath.

"What happened?"

He shakes his head "I don't know. Vandals. I don't know." He looks at me. "Why would anybody want to do this?"

"I don't know." The memory of Mr. Wood's angry face floats before me. "What are you going to do?"

"Clean up this mess, I reckon. I don't want the neighbors waking up to this." Suddenly, he looks old. Defeated.

"Let me help."

"No, you go on to work. Excuse me, Andrea." Mr. Fox turns away and walks into his house.

I think about the Foxes and Mr. Wood all day. I know he did it. When I get home, I'm tempted to go over there and confront him. But I don't have the guts. Instead, I pick at my supper of microwaved fish sticks, then go to bed early.

I can't get comfortable. I keep checking my clock radio. Eleven. Midnight. Then I hear a noise outside. It's coming from next door. I creep over to my bedroom window and peep out. Mr. Wood is piling burlap sacks in the bed of his truck. Then he gets in the vehicle and eases it down to the Foxes. I run for the closet and throw on a pair of jeans and shirt. Then I stop. This really isn't my business. What can I do? But I can't stand the picture of Mr. Fox, looking so forlorn. Picture. I grab my automatic camera and scramble out the door barefoot.

Mr. Wood squats and picks up one of the driveway rocks. I fumble with the camera, then squeeze the shutter, hoping the street lamp will fill in around the flash.

"What the hell--" Mr. Wood drops the rock. On his foot. "Damn!" He tries to grab for my camera. "You'd better give that here."

"You touch me and I'm going to scream loud enough to wake up every neighbor on this street. All I need is for one of them to call the police."

"You're not going to scream." Mr. Wood's face turns ugly and mean. "You make trouble for me, I'll make plenty more for you."

My heart falls into my stomach, but I stand there, clutching my camera like a weapon. I point to the little black box. "It won't cost much to make several copies of one shot. You even think about bothering the Foxes again, or me, and you're going to find yourself in the paper." My heart begins to climb out of my gut. " 'Town's Oldest Vandal.' Right beside the picture of the extension homemakers."

He runs his tongue over his lips and eyes me. "You're bluffing. You're scared of your own shadow."

He's right. I'm afraid. But now I'm mad, too. And I'm determined to make things right for my friends. "Tell you what," I say. "Let's both go home and think about it. I'll think about calling the police. You think about paying for the damage you've caused. If the Foxes tell me tomorrow some anonymous somebody left them money, I'll know our business is done." My stomach flops as I turn my back to him, but I walk away and return to my house.

My courage fails the moment I'm inside the door. I check the locks twice, then peep out the living room window, watching Mr. Wood sneak back into his truck and drive home. I wonder if I'll ever sleep again, worrying about whether Mr. Wood is slashing my tires or cooking up some other revenge. Then I surprise myself. To hell with him. Maybe he'd better start worrying about what I might do. I'm a grown woman. I'm capable of taking care of myself.

My cubicle never seemed so small before. I find myself trying to make small talk over the phone. I'm surprised at how many people want to make a connection, even to a stranger. Ed in Hinton tells me all about his wife and boys and how he sells NASCAR memorabilia for a living. "You've been mighty helpful, young lady," he says. "I'll be sure to do business with you folks again."

Work goes better than it ever has before, but I can't wait to get home. Right away, I see the mailbox, resting on a brand new post. Mr. Fox is carrying a can of paint. There's a new concrete birdbath. I jump out of my car and rush over. "You know, Andrea, this old world isn't so bad," he says. "I reckon somebody's conscience started aching, because this morning I found an envelope."

"Really?" I shoot a glance at Mr. Wood's house.

"There was enough money in there to take care of everything."

"That's wonderful."

"Yes, yes it is." Mr. Fox grins at me. "Maybe the whole thing was a blessing in disguise. I found something for Mother when I went to buy the birdbath. The store delivered it this afternoon." He sets the paint down and motions for me to follow him to the back yard.

It's something, all right. It's a huge, glassy purple ball cradled on a stone pedestal. I didn't know they still made those things. Thought they'd gone the way of the plastic pink flamingo. Mrs. Fox stands beside it, resting both hands on the lawn ornament.

"Look, Andrea, isn't this marvelous?" She strokes the violet sphere gently. "Look how it sparkles with light."

Obediently, I look. I see trees and flowers, and the dark reflections of Mr. and Mrs. Fox and myself. My hands stretch forth to touch the iridescent surface. Its smoothness comforts me. The twinkling violet draws me nearly into a trance. "It is marvelous," I say in wonder. I swear a mantle of shimmering light rises from the globe and envelopes this sweet old couple and myself.

Mr. Fox lays a hand on my shoulder. "Isn't it something how things always work out for the best?" The warmth from his hand spreads to my heart.

Fitting In

People think I'm dumb, but I'm not. I just can't help the way words pop out of me. Sometimes my brain feels like a pinball machine, with ideas slamming around, dinging and pinging. That's why I like to write. To get it all down. I could write a book real easy. I bet Oprah would love to read it. She might even invite me to be on her show.

I am so excited. I can't believe I'm at a real writers' conference. My mom just dropped me off at Cedar Lakes in Ripley. I wish I could have driven here myself. I am twenty-two, after all. But I just can't seem to concentrate on that driver's manual. I wouldn't let Mom stay with me, though. I heard her on the telephone before the conference, talking to somebody about looking out for me. That made me so mad. I'm not an idiot. I just play one on TV. Ha!

"Hi, what's your name?" says a woman at the registration table.

"Serena Jenkins."

The woman smiles at me and hands me a folder. There's a label with my name on it! "There you go. Everything you need is right in there."

Oh boy. Oh boy. Oh boy. I find a bench and dig inside the folder. It sure is hot. Wish I could go for a swim in that big old pond with the geese and ducks. I'm glad I wore shorts and a T-shirt. A lot of times, Mom has to buy me men's clothes to find a big enough size, but I don't care.

It doesn't matter to me what I wear. Wow, a nice, fresh yellow note pad. I like those pads with lines. I wish I had a computer, but then I don't know how to type. I bet I could learn real fast, though. Ooh, there's a name tag with "Serena" printed on it. There's the schedule. I jump up and go looking for the first classroom. My sandals make a funny whacking clacking on the pavement. Ugh. Goose mess.

I want to sit right up front, so I don't miss anything.

I can't wait. I can't wait. Thank goodness I brought my copy of *Little Women* with me. This is my favorite book of all time. *Little Men* is pretty good, too. Louisa May Alcott is my number one favorite writer of all time. That's where I got the idea of being a writer, from Jo. She always had a hard time settling down, too. The only time I can sit still is when I read.

Finally, we're getting started. The speaker is some woman from Virginia named Cheryl Connor. I never heard of her, but she looks nice. I wonder if any of her books have been made into movies, like *Little Women*. The person introducing Cheryl Connor says she has published a lot of novels and story collections, so I reckon she must be pretty good at writing. OK. OK. OK. I've got my notepad. Where's my pen? I dig in my purse. I swear I never can find anything when I want it. Oh, there it is. And a peppermint. It sure is hard sometimes to get that plastic wrapper untwisted. The boy next to me frowns. I guess he's having a bad day. I smile at him, but he doesn't smile back. The boys I knew in high school weren't friendly, either.

"Let's talk about structure," Cheryl Connor says. "Keep in mind that your story needs a beginning, middle and end."

"Are you going to take notes?" I ask the boy beside me. I peek at his notebook. "Oh, is that a poem? Did you write that?"

"Shhh," he says. He could have just told me yes or no.

Cheryl Connor goes on for a while, then asks, "Can somebody give me an example?"

"*Little Women*!" Shoot. I didn't mean to holler. I see people smiling at me in that way I hate. Like I'm stupid.

Cheryl Connor squints at my name tag. "Go ahead, Serena."

"Well, OK. See, the beginning is where you find out that the father is away at war and the family doesn't have much money. The middle is where the father gets sick and the mother has to leave, and then Beth gets sick, and everything is just awful. Things just keep getting worse and worse. Beth dies--" I stop and cover my mouth. "Oops, didn't mean to spoil it for you. Anyway, Jo tells Teddy she doesn't love him, and he gets mad. The end is where Meg gets married and Amy and Teddy fall in love and Jo ends up with the professor and it looks like everything is going to work out pretty good." Whew. I look around and I see a bunch of eyeballs staring at me.

"That's exactly right, Serena," Cheryl Connor says and smiles at me real nice. "You see in the beginning where, when and under what circumstances the story is taking place. Then the conflict escalates and intensifies in the middle. At the ending, there is a resolution, decisions are made." OK. So I'm not so stupid after all.

"Conflict is so important," Cheryl Connor says.

"Like when Amy burns Jo's manuscript and Jo won't forgive her and goes off skating without her and Amy falls through the ice!" This stuff isn't so hard.

"Yes, that's one example," Cheryl Connor says, then looks to the other side of the room and starts talking again. That woman sure has a lot to say. Finally, she asks, "Does anybody have any questions?"

I make sure to speak up real quick. "After I get done writing and send it off, how long before I get books in the mail?"

Cheryl Connor doesn't look at me. Instead she points to a woman with her hand in the air. "Do you ever use real people in your fiction?" the woman asks.

"I'm always observing people in real life," Cheryl Connor says. "I don't literally use real people, but I do draw inspiration from real life."

I'm afraid she didn't hear me before, so I holler, "What about my books?"

"Shhh!" the boy beside me hisses like a mean old cat. Then I look around and see everybody frowning at me. Cheryl Connor looks sad. I've done something wrong, but I don't know what. I guess I'd better keep my mouth shut.

In the lunch line, I try to talk to people. "So what do you like to write?" I ask the woman behind me. She looks really smart. I'd like to have eyeglasses hanging from a cord, too. I slide my tray past the salad. Ugh. Oh, hamburgers. I love hamburgers.

"Mostly fiction," the woman says.

"Making up stuff, you mean? Me, too. Like Louisa May Alcott. Hey, you want to sit together?"

"You go on," the woman says. "I'm not sure what I want."

"OK, I'll save you a seat."

But she doesn't sit beside me. She goes way over to the other side of the room. I wave at her. Maybe she doesn't see me. No, she sees me all right. I'm not stupid. Nobody will sit near me. I should have kept my big mouth shut in class. Mom is always telling me I need to calm down. The hamburger looks juicy, but the bite I'm chewing won't go down my throat. I'm not going to cry like some baby. I will not. I will not.

OK. I can start over. I'll try to do better, just like Amy. I'm going to pick up my tray and go sit with those three ladies about my mom's age. I bet they'll be nice to me. I'll be real quiet, like Beth, and maybe we'll end up trading addresses and I can show Mom I know how to make friends.

"Hi!" I set my tray on the table. My purse slips from my shoulder and when I try to catch it, I knock over my glass of milk. "Uh oh! Sorry!" I smile and start mopping up the mess with napkins. The ladies start mopping, too. Then they stand and start gathering their stuff. "You don't have to get up! I'll get this cleaned up in just a minute." I know I'm talking too fast and too loud.

"I need to make a call," one woman says and takes off. "Me, too," says another. The other one just shakes her head and walks away.

I sit down and smile, just in case anybody is looking at me. I take another bite of hamburger and try to swallow. My throat hurts. I will not cry. I will not. I will not.

"Who in the world let her into this conference?" A couple of girls about my age are talking at the table behind me. My heart starts thumping, but I try to chew my hamburger.

"Well, I guess it's a free country."

"Did you hear her in Cheryl Connor's class? Somebody ought to talk to her." Swallow. Swallow. Swallow.

"Just ignore her. It's obvious she's got developmental problems."

I get up and throw my lunch in the trash can. I may be stupid, but I have feelings just like anybody else. I'm going to find a pay phone and call Mom to come pick me up. Oh. I can't. She was going to shop and then pick me up at five. Well, I'll go to the afternoon session, but I won't say a word. I won't come back tomorrow. I don't want to write anymore.

I don't want to go into the classroom, but it's too hot to sit outside. "Let's talk about character," Cheryl Connor says. I won't take notes. I won't. I won't. "Before starting a story, I like to write down every single thing I can think of about the character."

"Like what?" says a guy. He didn't raise his hand.

"Her favorite book, religion, how she gets along with her family. Everything. I try to create a character so real that she walks around in my head." Cheryl Connor looks at her watch. "I want you all to think of a character, come up with a list of traits and then write a brief character sketch."

Everybody starts scratching with pencils and pens. I guess I might as well, too. I don't know what traits are, but I'm not about to ask. All I can think about is feeling so alone in that lunchroom. It reminds me of grade school, when nobody would play with me. That was so long ago, that little girl seems to be somebody separate from me. I feel so sorry for her. I start writing, bearing down so hard the pen punches right through the paper. I don't care. I'm just going to throw it away, anyway. Then Cheryl Connor says, "How about passing those to me?" She shuffles through them quickly. "We only have time for a few. Here we go." She holds up my holey paper. I bet she's going to read it just so everyone can laugh:

The little girl stood on the playground, watching the other children laughing and running and jumping. She didn't even try to talk to them. She had tried so many times before. Sometimes they laughed at her and ran away. Sometimes the boys pushed her, hard, and told her to leave them alone. The girls usually just ignored her. That hurt the most. She was different. But she didn't know how. If she didn't know, how could she ever fix herself so she could fit in?

Everybody in the class is so quiet. "May I ask who wrote this?" I start to raise my hand. Cheryl Connor turns to me, her face so kind that I think she might be an angel. "That is lovely. In just a few sentences, we enter this little girl's world and begin to care about her. Serena, I hope you continue with this. Please keep writing."

I will, Cheryl Connor. I will. I will. I will.

Full Bloom

Mother tried to cultivate me the way she did her roses. She pruned and crooned. She applied fertilizer generously. She watered with care.

The roses responded with grace. They developed into delicate, sweet-smelling ornaments. Mother would gently cup a pale pink blossom in her hand and breathe deeply of its fragrance. It was the only time I can remember seeing her with a peaceful expression.

Mother always looked distressed when her gaze fell upon me. Naming me after a flower failed to instill a single delicate trait. I was gangly and awkward, loud and dirty. "Oh, Lily," Mother said the time I brought a dead chipmunk into the house. I thought I could revive it by rinsing it in the kitchen sink.

If Mother were a flower, she wouldn't be a rose. She had no protective thorns. She was a hothouse orchid, elegant, but requiring tender care. Her face would fall into a sad frame whenever Dad teased her about her "flower foolishness" or laughed at her attempts to transform me into a civilized creature. "You're trying to domesticate a wildcat, Nell," he told her. Dad, who was in charge of transportation for the county's schools, treated Mother with fondness, but he never seemed to really listen to her. Behind her back, he encouraged my tomboy nature. He bought me a Swiss Army knife and showed me how to gut fish.

I wanted to be as worthy as the son I knew Dad would have preferred. I refused to allow myself to throw up when Dad made me watch him dress a deer. "You can learn from every situation," he told me. I listened and nodded my head as he explained the animal's anatomy.

But I wanted to please Mother, too. Sunday mornings, I stood silently while Mother brushed the knots out of my hair and made me wear flouncy dresses and socks with white lace at the ankles. She would smile, almost with happiness, as we approached our pew. But her efforts were about as effective as trying to tame kudzu by calling it ground cover. "Oh, Lily," she cried when she caught me behind the church, trying to strangle a boy named William with the sash I'd yanked from my dress. He'd committed the crime of telling me I looked pretty.

Dad won in the end. I became a surveyor, specializing in rural properties. Mother asked once if I owned anything other than cotton shirts, jeans and boots. "I've got khakis, too," I said, trying to stop my mouth from twitching.

I wanted to tell her that she had played a part in my career choice, but I didn't think she would understand. Most of my early memories centered on Mother's garden. When her back was turned as she mounded shredded mulch around her plants, properly outfitted with gardening gloves, I rooted barehanded through the rich dark stuff for interesting worms and bugs. I thought I was a big girl when she first allowed me to carry her watering can. There was no way I could have worked inside a building all day.

"Lily," she said the last time I visited, sitting at her kitchen table and drinking Earl Gray out of a pink-flowered china teacup, "If you don't learn how to act more feminine, you'll never find a husband and I'll never have grandchildren." She looked away, and I knew she was peering into some fantasy of her and the next generation in the rose garden. I wanted to say that meeting men was as easy as buying a six-pack. But I swallowed my smart remark.

"If only you'd wear your hair in a softer style." Mother reached over and touched my long braid. "It would be so becoming to your heart-shaped face."

I decided to create a diversion. "Are you competing in the flower show at the state fair this year?" I helped myself to an oatmeal cookie.

Mother brightened. "Oh, yes. I have a David Austin rose that is just stunning. It should just reach full bloom for the judging. I really think this is my year." She glanced at the clock on the wall and moved the plate of cookies away, just out of reach. Shouldn't ruin supper.

She had collected many ribbons over the years, but Mother had never won the big prize, the best of show. She never criticized the judges, just patiently waited for the next fair. "You'll come this year to see the display, won't you?"

Standing around and looking at flowers was not my idea of a good time. I tried to think of an excuse and was glad when Dad passed through the kitchen, catching our conversation.

"I guess that means another week of toast for breakfast and pasta for supper while Nervous Nell worries over her contenders," he said, grabbing three cookies from the plate. "I just don't see the point, but I reckon it's something to fill your time."

Tears formed in Mother's pale blue eyes, but she said nothing. Dad headed out of the kitchen, pausing to pat Mother's shoulder without really looking at her. "You want to watch the game?" he asked me.

I knew I'd end up at the fair.

I plowed a path among the other fairgoers, sweating in the August humidity as I rushed to the West Virginia Building to meet Mother for the judging. I just about wrecked a stroller, trying to dodge two women waving their corn dogs as they chatted. I nearly crashed into an old man on a walker, but a pocket of space opened and I veered around him.

I hurried inside the exhibit building, whipping past the quilts and baked goods. I was late. The judges had finished their work, festooning the arrangements with yellow, red and blue ribbons. I could see Mother standing quietly before her rose, her hands folded before her. She wore a pink blouse colored like a quiet sunset and white pants that looked like linen but weren't wrinkled.

"Whoa," I said. There was no ribbon, not even an honorable mention, and I could see why. The once-glorious David Austin rose drooped forlornly in its vase. "What happened?"

Mother pointed to the vase. There was a gap of about an inch between the water and the tip of the stem. "Someone tipped it over by accident, I guess." Then I saw the wet spot on the cloth napkin beneath the glass. "I don't think they realized how much water had spilled when they set it back." The rose didn't have a chance in a building with no air conditioning. Anyone else would have been demanding an explanation or screaming sabotage, but not Mother.

"Look, we'll hunt up a judge and explain the situation. Maybe we can run back to the house and--"

"No," Mother said. "I'm not going to make a scene." She looked at her watch. "Besides, your father will be here any minute. We're working the Chicken Shack for Rotary this evening."

I heard Dad whistling before I saw him. He frowned at the sight of the David Austin rose. "Tough break," he said. "Better luck next year, Nell."

"No," Mother said, her voice as soft and thin as the petals dropping from the rose. "This is my last show."

"You don't mean that." I couldn't remember a fair without Mother entering the flower show.

"Well, it's not the end of the world," Dad said. He was trying to find something helpful to say, but he might as well have lit a match to gasoline.

"That's right," Mother said. "It's just foolishness."

"Don't take it so hard," Dad said. "It's just one flower."

Mother turned on Dad and I was surprised to see the gentle blue of her eyes could harden into ice. I wondered just how much Mother had struggled to contain herself over the years. "You see the effort I put into that garden year after year and you don't understand what it means to me?" She had raised her voice only a little, but Mother stopped and glanced around as though she expected to be restrained by security.

Now Dad was getting his back up. "I go to work every day, year after year. Nobody hands me a ribbon for getting the kids to and from school, and I don't expect one." I hunched my shoulders and balled my hands in my jeans pockets.

"But you get paid. Your career is your ribbon, proof of your competence." She picked up the vase that had belonged to her mother and dropped it in the nearest trash can. "This was my chance to do one right thing."

And then she was gone, slipping away while we stared at the garbage can. I dug into the bin, held up the broken pieces and dropped them back in. "I can't believe she did that."

"Does this have something to do with menopause?" Dad asked.

Trying to find someone on the crowded fairgrounds was like trying to locate a property marker in a thicket of greenbrier. We circled around the West Virginia building a couple of times. We checked the exhibits at the Grandstand. I covered the women's restrooms, squatting to quickly check the shoes peeking from the bottom of the stall doors. No snowy white sneakers. Then I joined Dad again and we lapped the midway of rides and games. I didn't really think Mother would be whirling or spinning through the air, but I tried to scan every seat in motion.

"I'm supposed to be at the Chicken Shack in half an hour," Dad said, rattling the change in his pocket. He always did that at home when he thought Mother and I were taking too long to get ready. And always the pocket of his right leg, his bad leg. "We're not accomplishing anything, just chasing our tails."

"You're right," I said. "Let's stop and think. I bet Mother has tried to find some quiet spot. Maybe she's at the animal exhibits."

We headed for the barns, cruising past the stalls of horses and cows. The air swelled with the pungent smell of straw and manure. I paused in front of one of the stalls in the sheep barn. Some kid was trying to feed the core of a candy apple to a freshly shorn ewe, a pretty little Cheviot that looked as French as its breed sounded. Just as I was trying to decide whether to say something to him, the sheep nibbled at a finger as it eagerly sought the apple. The boy shrieked, yanked his hand away and ran off.

The startled ewe tried to cough, then began to choke. Then it made no sound at all. Its eyes bulged with fright. Several people by now had stopped. "Better find the owner," someone said.

One look into that animal's panicked eyes told me there was no time for finding help. Someone had to do something now. I leapt over the wooden gate and into the stall. I wrapped my arms around the ewe and tried the Heimlich maneuver, but my efforts weren't having any effect on the struggling animal. I was probably just punching the poor creature's gut.

"Tracheotomy," Dad said, standing on the other side of the stall and fumbling in his pocket. Hell of a time to be rattling his change.

"What?" I grunted.

Dad reached into a pocket and pulled out his Swiss army knife.

"Are you kidding?"

"That animal doesn't have much time." It had stopped fighting me and lay limply in my arms. The other sheep, sensing trouble, began to bleat with fear.

I'd probably be sued, and I had no idea what kind of diseases I might be exposing myself to, but I grabbed the knife from Dad. I opened a blade and slit the sheep's throat. Blood stained the freshly-washed wool, but there was also the sound of air.

"A tube," Dad said. "You need a tube."

I looked around, desperately trying to think of what could serve as a breathing tube. And then I saw Mother in the crowd. "May I have that?" she calmly asked a woman holding a super-sized soft drink. The woman looked confused. Mother yanked the straw from the cup. "Thank you." She leaned over the stall and handed it to me.

I stuck the straw in the hole I'd cut and held it in place with my hands. Incredibly, the animal began to breathe. And to resist. The air stank from the smell of the thing soiling itself. I struggled to keep the straw in place. "I could use some help here." Dad looked at me helplessly. The gate to the stall was locked, and there was no way he could climb it with that bad leg. I tried to make eye contact with a couple of young men in World Wrestling Federation shirts, but they turned their heads from me.

And then my mother, whose primary exercise was stooping or squatting to tend her flowers, began to scale the gate. She was stuck straddling the top until my dad, without a word, went to her and helped her over.

Mother knelt beside me. "What do you need?"

"You hold this straw in place, I'll keep her from thrashing around." As Mother's hands reached to replace mine, a spurt of blood splattered her pink blouse and white pants. She started, then just closed her hands around the wound and applied more pressure.

We didn't look up until the owner and a vet arrived and shooed us out of the stall. The farmer was especially grateful to the soft drink woman, who was explaining to him her brilliant idea of using the straw. Dad was staring at Mother as though he'd never seen her before.

"Nice assist, Nell." He draped his arm around her and squeezed her shoulder.

Mother looked at her bloody hands. "All those things," she murmured.

"What?" Dad asked.

"All those things you taught Lily. It saved that animal's life." Mother wiped her hands on her stained pants.

"I'm afraid those clothes are ruined," I said.

"They're just clothes," said the woman who used to iron my underwear and beg me to stay out of mud puddles on the way to the school bus stop. She looked up from blood-splattered sneakers to me. "There are more important things than clothes. Or roses."

The woman who stood before me, covered in blood and excrement, had spent a lifetime attempting to bring beauty and order to her world. "Roses are important," I said. "I tried to help because I was brought up by a mother who cares." I stared my challenge right at her. "A woman who keeps trying, who doesn't give up."

Mother dropped her head and considered her filthy hands for a long time before those tender blue eyes met mine again. "Well, look at you," she finally said.

"I know I'm a mess," I said, using the back of my dirty hand to brush the loose hair from my face.

"No," Mother said. "You're in full bloom."

Real Estate

"You want to put a hold on it?" Otis Gwinn, the real estate agent, reaches for the pen in his shirt pocket. His appearance reminds me so much of my dad. The way he rubs the back of his nearly bald head. His cheeks, etched by the sun into crevices. Jenna even got confused and called him Grandpa on the drive over. Dad, though, would have required at least a dozen Dr. Peppers to reach Otis's intensity. I miss my folks. Melanoma. Breast cancer. And now Don. At night, I lie awake from a foolish fear that if I love Jenna too much, she'll be taken from me, too.

Jenna stands in the middle of the empty living room, her eyes closed, her thin arms thrust out as though she intends to gather the air. Slowly, slowly, my little girl turns, making one complete circle.

Otis looks over his checklist. "This is a great value for a two-story house, Mrs. Martin." hc says. "You got municipal water and sewer. For heat, you got a gas boiler with hot water radiators. Very comfortable in the winter." Not so agreeable in August, though. I feel sweat inching down my back. Otis scans his list again. "That vinyl siding is only three years old. So, Faith, you mind if I call you Faith? What do you think? One of the other agents is bringing somebody here this afternoon."

I hesitate. This is only the first house that we've looked at, and it smells a little of mildew. But I feel panic grabbing my gut. Maybe I'd better take what I know I can afford. I wish Don was here to tell me what to do. How can he be gone? He was too young to have a heart attack. I know he was carrying too much weight, like me. But I tried to take care of my family, baking the chicken instead of frying it, fixing fresh salads. I didn't buy those convenient boned, skinless chicken packages, either. We were saving our money to buy some land in Greenbrier County and build our own house.

Jenna stands as motionless as a fairy statue, her eyes still closed and her arms outstretched. I'm not sure that at age five she understands her daddy really is gone. Don wanted to give us everything. "Nothing but the best for my girls," he said so many times. He was working two jobs, one at the plant and another as a caretaker on a horse farm. "Hard work never killed anybody," he said, always calm and sure of himself. Now that he's gone, Jenna and I have to move and make room for the new caretaker. I went back to work after Jenna started kindergarten, but even now with my job as a bookkeeper and the insurance money, I worry about making mortgage payments.

The grinding gears of a dump truck make me start. I'm not used to the sounds of traffic. The noise seems to wake Jenna. She lowers her arms and looks at me with Don's moss-green eyes. "Daddy says this isn't the place for us."

She's been saying things like this for the past month, as though Don were whispering in her ear. It spooks me, but I figure this is her way of grieving. She has always been a child filled with imaginings, telling me about conversations between the horses on the farm. I wish I had a sense of Don's presence. I can't feel anything.

Otis cocks an eyebrow at her. "Now, why do you reckon your daddy wouldn't like this house?"

Jenna points through the hallway to the kitchen. "There's a problem with those pipes." Where in the world did she come up with a notion like that? Probably from sitting in Don's lap while he watched one of those public television home repair shows.

Otis coughs and spits out a sort of laugh. "Well, now, it seems to me that the problem here is you gals don't want to live right in town. I got a better place in mind." He heads outside.

"Come on, Jenna." I herd her to the door, my hand playing with that pretty long hair hanging down the back of her bib overalls. The brown hair she got from me, but those curls are Don's gift.

We climb into Otis's red Suburban and rumble from Ronceverte to Lewisburg. I don't like the way he drives with one hand, using the other to point to this house and that one, telling me the prices and circumstances of each sale. He flicks a bony index finger at a brick ranch. "Fellow there, younger than me, just up and died. His wife took off to Florida." The finger leaps again, like a divining rod. "UPS man lives there. His wife left him. I figure he'll decide to sell that place one of these days." Divorce. Nursing home. Death. I wonder if every real estate transaction has its roots in loss.

"This is a great neighborhood," he says as we skirt around the city, winding along streets of well-landscaped brick ranches. They're awfully close to each other. "Now, you're going to pay a little more, but it's a good investment. Whoops, here it is." The Suburban lurches onto a paved driveway.

Otis snags an apple from a tree in the yard, and hands another one to Jenna. They're munching like cows as we enter the house. I know the owner, even though I've never met her and she's not home. She's an elderly widow, very tidy. There's not one sign of a man's messiness. The beds are made with fluffy white coverlets. Grandchildren grin from neatly lined-up frames in the living room. The kitchen smells of cinnamon. Otis carelessly drops the core of his apple on a counter. I grab a paper towel, wrap the core with Jenna's half-eaten fruit and deposit the bundle in the trash can, which I knew I would find under her sink.

"Check out this basement." Otis leads us down into a huge cavern. I hate basements. I don't know why, exactly. Maybe it's because there's always a slight smell of decay, even in a well-maintained house like this one. "This really adds value."

Jenna stands silently, her head cocked like a beagle listening for the faint rustlings of a rabbit.

"Well? What do you think, Faith?" Otis asks me.

"It's very nice," I say.

"You want to buy it?" That hand is creeping for the pocket.

"Daddy says this isn't the place for us," Jenna says quietly.

Otis folds his arms across his chest. "What's wrong with this one?"

"The foundation." Her eyes beg me to believe her.

I can't name a reason, but I don't feel good about this house, either. The crevices in Otis's face are sliding into a sour expression. Before he can make a comment, I ask, "Do you have anything just a little further from town?"

The lines stretch into something of a smile. "Frankford," he says. "You gals want to go to Frankford." The belts on the Suburban squeal happily as we head north. Again, he drives with one hand, using the other to dial his cell phone, trying to reach the listing agent. He runs a red light, sailing through an angry blast of car horns.

"Stop the car!" My nerves are shot.

"What?" He's still trying to punch numbers into the phone.

"Pull over right now." He jerks the vehicle into the parking lot of Arby's. I open my mouth, wondering if I can spit out the stern words before I break down. "If you can't pay attention to your driving, we're not going to do business." Jenna's eyes are round and wide. She's not used to this tone of voice from me.

His face reddens with anger. "I've been driving a few more years than you have--"

"What if those cars hadn't waited? Don't you care that there's a child sitting beside you?" Then I start sobbing. The other day I broke down just because I saw a truck parked in the front of the post office and a man who was not Don got in it and drove off.

"Well, of course, I care," the old man says. "I got grandchildren and great-grandchildren." The red drains from his face. "I'm sorry. I just get wound up and forget myself." He eases the Suburban into traffic.

Jenna pipes up, "Both hands on the wheel."

"Yes, ma'am." He laughs and wraps his tanned, lined hands around the steering wheel. He drives past the fast food restaurants that give way to branch banks, which yield to tractor dealerships. We arrive at Frankford just about the time we've lost sight of commerce. Otis turns down a side road and pulls up to a pasture that's been divided into small lots for a housing development. He points to a nearly-new, Victorian-style farmhouse, painted a pretty pale yellow, sitting on maybe two acres.

The Suburban crunches along the gravel driveway. Already, I like this house and this place. "This isn't my listing, but they won't mind us looking," he says as we get out and approach the front door. There's a nice wrap-around porch. I could see myself sitting here, stringing green beans while Jenna plays with her dolls. He tries to slip a credit card past the lock. "Well, hell." Then he starts checking the windows. Jenna waits, humming to herself. "Here we go," he says, waving at the window he just pried open.

"Are you sure this is all right?"

"Absolutely." With a couple of grunts, he eases his thin frame through the opening. Jenna holds her arms up to him without hesitation and he hauls her inside. I drag myself in, too. My blouse sticks to my back.

These folks didn't live here very long. There's only one small scratch on the wood floor in the living room. Light skips across the freshly painted white walls and warms the oak-trimmed doorways. Jenna and I wander while Otis talks on his cell phone. Three bedrooms, two baths. It's really more than we need, but it's so pretty. One of the bedrooms has a perfect view of a pond, a gray weathered barn and golden rolls of baled hay. I could find peace here. I know I could.

Otis joins us and starts rubbing the back of his head. "I might as well tell you now that I don't think you're going to want this house." Jenna kneels at the big window and rests her arms on the sill. "The couple here, their child . . ." He won't look at me. "Leukemia. . ."

I try to blink away the tears, but they're coming regardless of my embarrassment. I don't know whether I'm crying for those parents or for my own disappointment.

Jenna turns around and stands. "Don't cry, Mommy. Daddy says this is the place for us."

I wipe my face with my other hand and look into the solemn face of my baby. "I don't think so, Jenna. This is a sad house."

She shakes her head, sending those dark curls flying. "No, Mommy. This house likes little kids."

Otis stares at me. All I can think to say is, "It's time for us to be getting back." Jenna leads us downstairs, her hand comfortably gliding along the oak stair railing.

Outside, we climb into the Suburban. No one speaks. A couple of miles down the highway, Otis suddenly brakes and turns down a side road. His right hand flies from the steering wheel and braces Jenna against the bench seat. "Sorry about that," he says. "I've got one more thing to show you." After a few miles, the yellow striping on the asphalt disappears. The road rises and narrows until it seems as though we're riding the spine of some great creature.

I can't imagine living anywhere this isolated. Just as I'm about to ask Otis to turn around, he pulls off onto the gravel shoulder. I don't see anything but thickly packed trees and a hint of a mountain range in the distance. He gets out and motions for us to follow him along a weedy path. I feel more uneasy with every beer bottle and cigarette butt I encounter. I wouldn't want to be out here after dark. The path bends, then suddenly reveals a rock outcropping, the gray stone marred by bright yellow and red spray-painted graffiti.

Beyond this edge of ugliness, though, lies beauty. The Greenbrier River cuts a great chasm far below the woody cliff where I stand, wrapping around the green-studded hill across from me like a horseshoe. Beyond the water, fold after fold of blue mountains reveal the layers of West Virginia.

"If you think this is something, come on over here." Otis jumps across a cleft to stand on the rim of the rock ledge. "If an old man can do it, you can, too." He holds his arms out for Jenna. It's a small rift, but a misstep could have fatal consequences. "We're fine right here," I say, just as a small figure darts from my side. I scream to Jenna, but I'm too late. She jumps, blindly believing.

Leaping after her without thinking, I somehow find myself right at the edge of the cliff, but standing. Jenna rests in Otis's arms, her arms around his neck.

I don't know which of them to start lecturing first. I'll decide as soon as my heart settles back into my blouse, now soaked under my arms. I've got to make sure that Jenna understands that she has to be careful, that the world is full of dangers. I reach for my daughter and take her from Otis into my arms.

"You can see into forever from here," he says. He turns to speak into the great space beyond the outcropping, not looking at me. "I come here sometimes when I get to thinking about my boy. We lost him in Vietnam."

"I'm sorry."

"You never really accept it, but you get used to it after awhile," he says, still talking at the sky. "You take comfort where you can, seeing his girl grow up to be so much like him, just as handy with a wrench as he was." He rubs the back of his head.

I hug Jenna closer to me. Her soft skin presses against my cheek, her curls smelling of apple-scented shampoo. When Don washed her hair, he would announce he was going to turn her into a brontosaurus. Then he'd lather Jenna's hair into crazy spikes of suds that made her giggle and squeal.

Jenna whispers in my ear, "Can we have the house, Mommy?"

"How much is the house, Mr. Gwinn?" I frown at the figure he names. I do the math in my head. Even if I offer ten percent less, and even if I can snag a favorable loan rate, it won't be easy to make ends meet.

"Can we, Mommy?" Her sweet voice penetrates my fear. I can't live my life this way, hesitating before every step. If I budget carefully, we can make it. I'll stretch my haircuts from six to eight weeks. I'll buy more store brands at the grocery. We'll plant snapdragons instead of renting videos. I answer her question with a squeeze.

A cooling breeze approaches, wrapping around us and drying the perspiration on my face. Jenna's lips curve into a smile. A genuine smile, something I haven't seen in weeks. "Daddy's here," she says.

"How do you know, Jenna?"

"The preacher said at the funeral that Daddy was closer to God," Jenna says. "And this is where God lives, in the sky and in the mountains."

The breeze flows around us, playing with Jenna's curls. I close my eyes and open myself to its embrace.

Hauling Evelyn

I wish everybody would quit hassling me. I'll do something about Evelyn eventually. My great Aunt Wanda says it's sacrilegious to haul Evelyn around in a bucket in the trunk of my car. It's not a bucket. It's a black plastic container, like heavy-duty Tupperware. I've started locking the Impala, because I wouldn't put it past Wanda to try to swipe Evelyn.

My friends think I'm weird and refuse to ride with me. They don't understand. None of them do. The rest of my life depends upon what I do with these ashes. My sister's been calling the shots all my life, and if I'm not careful, this will just give her an excuse to tighten her grip.

Right now, she's not giving me any trouble at all, wedged in the trunk between a jug of kitty litter and a box of old clothes I keep meaning to take to the women's shelter. Not even a rattle when I stop to pick up the kids. God, I'm glad they're back in school. I barely have time to roll down the window when Rocky comes running, with another boy right behind him.

"Mom, he don't believe me!" Rocky shouts in my face. I need to trim those bangs. He's as shaggy as a bear cub. Smells like one, too, on this warm September afternoon.

"He says you drive around with a dead person in your trunk!" Rocky's classmate has a buzz cut. I wonder if lice have already started making the rounds in school.

"That's right." I point to Rocky. "You. In the car. Now."

"You're lying," the other boy says. "Open up your trunk and let me see."

It's that special time of the month, and I'm just not in the mood. "If I have to get out and open up that trunk, I might just stick you in there, too." Little Buzz Cut takes off.

Rocky slides in the back seat and starts with this horsy snickering he's picked up in fourth grade. "Mom, you're so weird."

"Thank you."

Conan shuffles his way to the car and gets in. "Scoot over," he orders his little brother.

In the rear view mirror, I see Rocky trying to stretch his body the length of the bench seat. "You get up front with Mom."

"I said *scoot over*!" When Conan doesn't get what he wants, he just gets louder. And I hate to say this about my own child, but he's got a whiny voice that just wears on a person. His stringy dark hair needs trimmed, too.

Twisting around, I tell them, "Settle down. Both of you. Rocky, sit up." I turn back and look for my daughter. She's just in sixth grade, but she's already starting to act like we're aliens that abducted her from her real, normal family. There she is, with one of her girlfriends, pretending she doesn't see this long, menthol-blue sedan.

"Leia, you get your butt over here right now!" She skulks over to the car and jumps in beside me before I can holler something even more embarrassing. I turn over the ignition and ease the Impala into traffic.

Rocky starts snickering. "Yeah, Leia, get your big butt over here."

"No, your *humongous, gargartuan* butt!" Conan shouts.

"Mom, make them stop it," she says.

"Boys, settle down." I wonder if I need to stop at the store for milk.

"He started it," Conan says.

Conan. Rocky. Leia. No way you can have normal kids when you name them after movie characters. My moon-faced Conan's a whiner. Rocky is a little squirt. Leia, now, has every bit of a princess attitude. The names were my ex-husband's bright idea. I would have liked to name the boys Joseph and Ronald, nice respectable names. And to give my daughter my name, Susanna. And not shortened to Suzy, either. Evelyn got to keep her three syllables, but nobody could be bothered to use my full name.

Evelyn had the perfect life. It started with our hair. Same blonde color, but mine was stringy, like Conan's. Evelyn's hair just seemed to form ringlets. The fact that she was younger than me made it worse. "Look how neatly your sister colors," Mom would say. "Why do you have to grind your crayons like that?" Evelyn had the best grades, the right friends.

I could buy a carton of Virginia Slims if I had a nickel for every time my parents said, "Why can't you be more like Evelyn?" But I don't smoke anymore, even though I want to. Evelyn made me give up cigarettes. "Suzy, you don't really want to give your children cancer with that second-hand smoke, do you, hon?" Evelyn's voice was as smooth as silk, and as strong, too. My kids listened to her, always answered her, "Yes, Ma'am." Leia even cut her hair to look like Evelyn's, a short style with lots of body that lies just right.

Evelyn went steady with the same nice boy all through high school, married him and became a doctor's wife. He died a hero in the Gulf War when he went over with the National Guard. I was the one sneaking cigarettes and dating delinquents. At least Ronnie married me when I got pregnant with Leia. I'd like to know where he is now. I could barely afford to buy the kids a few new things for school, and I don't know what I'm going to do when they outgrow their winter coats. Oh, that's right. Evelyn set up a trust fund for them. She wasn't about to let me handle her money. No, she chose a banker instead of her own sister to make decisions about her niece and nephews. So I'm going to have to say pretty-please to some stranger whenever I want something for my kids. She's determined to dog me the rest of my life, even if she'll never again get to say, "Are you really going to wear that dress, hon? Out in public?"

"*Quit it*!" Conan yells.

"You quit it!" Rocky hollers back.

In the rear-view mirror, I can see them wrestling. I pull over, turn around and then I see they've unbuckled their lap belts. "You get those seat belts on right now," I scream. "If I ever catch you not wearing those belts, no videos for a month. And I mean it." Leia doesn't say a word, just stares out the passenger window. She's wearing enough Vanilla Fields to freshen an entire room.

That was the one thing in her life that Evelyn failed to do right. She wasn't wearing a seat belt when that dump truck drove through a stop sign and crashed into her car. She was on her way to church to play the organ for Wednesday evening services, so I figure she didn't want to wrinkle her linen dress. I saw her body at the hospital. I wanted to see it. I thought, somehow, the experience would set me free, but it didn't. Bloodied and broken as she was, she still had power in her. I think it bothered me most that her hair wasn't even messed up. And she still smelled nice. She always wore some kind of light cologne that reminded me of oranges and lemons.

"Go pick up my peach-colored suit at the house," she ordered me, though her mouth was closed. "That would be just right for the viewing. You don't mind doing that for me, do you, hon?"

So I had her cremated right away. Wanda had a fit, but it was over and done before she knew anything about it. Then she lit into me for not having a service, but I just couldn't endure a long tribute to Evelyn. I got some calls from the people at her church, too. I told them to go ahead and have a service themselves if they wanted one so bad. What people don't realize is that guilt trips don't work on somebody like me. When you can't please anybody, you quit trying.

"Mom."

"What, Rocky?"

"Mom, how come you burned Aunt Evelyn?" I look in the rear-view mirror and I see that his face is serious.

Leia snorts. "You are so ignorant. She was cremated."

"What's cremated?" Rocky asks.

"*Burned*!" Conan shouts.

"So, how come you did that?" Rocky asks.

"Be-cause," Leia says, drawing out the word like she's talking to somebody that's a saucer short of a place setting, "Mom couldn't afford to bury her."

"Where did you hear that?" I ask her.

"Nowhere. But we never have money for anything." I hear accusation in her voice and I want to slap her, to let her know she ought to be mad at her no-good father who won't pay child support. Count to ten, count to ten.

"Mom." It's Rocky again.

"What?"

"Are you just going to keep her in the trunk forever?"

"No." I wish I could. Evelyn is secure right where she is, and out of sight, too.

"Well, what are you going to do with her?"

"I don't know, Rocky." Wanda wants me to put her in a big metal urn, right between Mom and Dad's stones. No way. Evelyn might be as harmless as talcum powder, but I can't take that chance.

Powder. Laundry powder dissolves in water. Seems to me that Evelyn should, too. Then I'd be free. "Hey, kids," I say. "You want to go to Bluestone Lake?"

"Right now?" Leia says.

"Yeah!" Rocky answers.

"*Yes! Yes! Yes*!" Conan bellows.

"Why?" Leia wants to know, suspicious. "Mom! You can't just go and dump her ashes."

"I don't see why not." I keep on driving.

"All right," Rocky says.

"Fish food," says Conan.

I nose the Impala down the narrow access road to the parking area at the lower level of the big concrete dam. I could have gone to Bluestone Lake Park, but the water's too calm there. Evelyn might just float on the surface. The water streaming through the dam should mix those particles up pretty well.

The boys jump out of the car, race toward the railing and start a spitting contest. Leia just sits there. "I'm not getting out."

"Suit yourself." I step out and stretch. It's one of those days when summer is about to give way to autumn. It's hot, the mountains are green, but you can just feel in the air that everything is about to change.

I open up the trunk and I start to lose my nerve. I know good and well that Evelyn would want a better send off than this. Something with some dignity. It wasn't her fault that she was perfect. Maybe I should go and order that urn. I've lived in her shadow all this time. I'm used to it.

I hear the passenger door shut and I look up to see Leia watching me. "Aunt Eveyln wouldn't do this to you."

I nod. I don't want to cry.

"She said she'd take me to the Sears portrait studio if I didn't like my school pictures." Leia squeezes her eyes against the slant of the afternoon sun. "I don't guess that's going to happen now."

I don't answer. Once, I was just the lesser sister and daughter. Now I'm the not-quite-good-enough mother. Just as I'm about to close the trunk, the boys rush over to me. Conan reaches in and grabs the plastic bucket. "OK, let's do it."

Before I can say anything, Rocky pounces on him. "No, I want to carry Aunt Evelyn."

"*No, me*," Conan growls. "She liked me better than you."

"Did not." Rocky tugs on the lid.

"Did *too*." Conan clutches the black container tighter to his chest.

Leia shakes her head in disgust. "If anybody was her favorite, it was me."

I snatch the bucket from my son. "Give me that." To hell with spreading Evelyn's ashes. I'm going to pitch the whole damn thing into the water. She can just sink to the bottom.

Just as I'm raising my arms, Leia yells, "Mom, don't!" Too late. The container sails threw the air. And bounces against the iron railing. I can't do anything right. The lid flies off and Eveyln escapes, soaring all around us. And she's not pretty talcum powder. More like ashes from a fireplace.

Evelyn rains on us. Leia plucks a piece from her hair and drops it with a scream. “Oh my God, it’s a bone!” She shudders and her sandal crunches another bit of Evelyn.

The children shake themselves like wet dogs and stare at the ashes and fragments around me. I can’t move. I’m coated with Evelyn. I swear I can smell lemons and oranges. I feel my sweaty pores opening and absorbing the essence of my sister. There’s nothing I can do about it.

I hear laughter. More like hysterical giggling. I start to fuss at the kids, then I realize the noise is coming from me. I can’t stop. I collapse on a nearby bench, the laughter rolling out of me in big waves, like sobs. Maybe I am sobbing.

“Mom, are you all right?” Leia’s standing right beside me, but her voice sounds far away.

“Mom?” I can’t seem to focus on Rocky’s swimming face.

“*Mom*!” I turn to Conan and I start to come to myself.

“What is it, hon?” I feel calm, for the first time in years. Maybe ever.

Conan looks at me uncertainly. “Are you OK?”

“I’m fine.” I see the doubt on the children’s faces. “Look at this mess! Let’s get this cleaned up.” I walk over to the Impala, root around in the trunk and find an old windshield scraper/brush. I squat and quickly sweep the ashes over the pavement edge and into the water. “Ashes to water,” I say and smile.

“Mom, can I keep the bucket?” Rocky asks.

“*No*, I want it!” Conan shouts.

I lay my hands on their shoulders. “You don’t want to carry on like this, do you? In public?” I pick up the container and lid and drop them in the trash can by the bench.

The children look at me like they've never seen me before. Silently, they get in the car and buckle up.

I finish my job, shut the trunk and slide in the driver's seat. "I bet all of you are hungry. How would you like to stop at Kirk's for burgers?"

"I'm not really hungry," Leia says.

"I know you're hot. Let me treat you to a soda, anyway." I look over and can't believe I never noticed that sloppy posture before. "And Leia, hon, sit up straight."

Leia scoots a little closer to the passenger door, but she sits up. "Yes, ma'am."

"You boys good to go?"

"Yes, ma'am," they say together.

"That's fine." I pull my blouse from the seat belt so it won't wrinkle so badly. Then I check my hair in the rearview mirror. Tomorrow, I'll make an appointment with the stylist. "That's just fine."

Bittersweet

I'm not bitter. I don't sit around trying to figure out how a fair property settlement leaves me with a Honda Civic and Karl with a BMW. "I'd have made sure I got that BMW if I was you," said my best friend Bev. But I don't worry about the cars, or the shiny new Toyota Land Cruiser that he uses to show clients West Virginia's prime mountaintop acreage.

Bev warned me to watch out when she learned that he secured the services of a law firm with a dozen names. She and Karl both work at the economic development office. "Caroline, he is so clueless," she cackled. "I started off asking Karl how he was doing, and then I just kept digging." My lawyer was renovating a little house for an office. He was real nice, handing me tissues while I cried and wondered if any of this would have happened if we'd had children. I didn't want to be vindictive, I sniffed. I just wanted to make a fresh start.

That's just what I tried to do. I couldn't stay in Princeton, worrying about running into Karl every time I went to the bank or grocery store. So I moved to a little community in Monroe County where I could hear roosters calling for the morning.

The peace of the country soothes me, but I do miss the cosmetic counter at Penney's. I always sold more product than the other clerks. Most of them made the mistake of wearing too much makeup themselves. Seeing those perfectly lined and colored masks just intimidated customers. And some of those clerks thought good service meant standing at attention, staring without a smile. The customers thought they were snobs.

I always dressed in soft tones, which look nice with my blonde hair, anyway. Maybe I'd add a hint of color with a scarf. I'd wear small gold earrings, no clanky bracelets. And I'd wear a quiet fragrance, sometimes just lotion with a touch of a floral scent, like freesia. That's how I got the shy customers, the ones that wanted to treat themselves, but were afraid. They usually didn't even see me at first as they edged closer to the counter, eyeing the lipsticks and lotions. "Hi, how are you today?" I'd say quietly. When they looked up in surprise, I'd quickly smile and make some comment to connect us. "You know, navy is a perfect color for your skin tone," I said to one young woman in a dark T-shirt and jeans. She was herding two boys past my counter toward the exit, but I saw that look of longing. The other clerks had mini-strokes, but I seated the boys -- named Conan and Rocky, after movie characters -- on the high stools and let them paint each other's faces with a tube of Rose Mist while I tended to their mother. She bought a complete makeover.

The commute became too expensive when I moved to the country. So now I'm working at a local drugstore, ringing up prescription medicine, magazines and chewing tobacco. It saddens me to accept money for a beige foundation when I know how good the customer would look in the Cream Ivory I used to sell. But I try not to be bitter. Even when I heard that Karl had $1,200 to blow on a purebred English Bulldog puppy. "I wouldn't live with a dog in the house," Bev said when she passed on that tidbit. "Especially not with my antique chairs." I don't know which surprised me most, the money or his acceptance of responsibility for a living creature.

I kind of wish Bev wouldn't feel obligated to report every move Karl makes. She was the one who introduced us, so maybe she feels she has to stay involved. She calls long-distance from the office. After she gives the Karl update, she tells me what I ought to be doing. "You'll never meet another man out there in the boondocks." Sometimes, I wish I could leave Bev, too. But I swear it's easier to get a divorce than it is to pry loose from a friendship. At least it's been a few weeks since she called to tell me he took a vacation in Wyoming. I'd like to know when he became Nature Boy. I never could get him to even take a walk with me.

Wonder where he's getting all this extra pocket change. It could be that his grandmother left him some kind of inheritance when she died. From the simple way she lived, nobody could tell whether she had money or not. The only hint of prosperity I ever saw was an expensive-looking cameo pin that she wore to church every Sunday. "I wonder who got that pin?" Bev asked the other day.

I don't know, but other than that pin handed down from her mother's mother, I do know she hated to accept gifts. "I don't need a thing," she always said. When I'd take her to JC Penney to spend the gift certificate Karl and I got her for her birthday, I'd try to steer her to a pretty blouse or a good brand of night cream. "I like to use bear grease," she'd joke, and instead buy something for one of her grandchildren.

I don't go to the mall much now. I always avoid JC Penney. I just can't stand to see those looks of pity, layered over relief that it's not them. Today, though, I needed to go to Sears, where I'm trying to find a gasoline-powered generator. It's too early in the season, the young salesman tells me. "You're not going to find that kind of thing in August," he says.

He doesn't understand that death is in the air. It's still hot, but the season is changing. I can see it, smell it, feel it. The humidity is diminishing, summer's languidness replaced by brittleness as the sun shines more harshly, casting sharper shadows and baking the life out of the landscape. I panicked when I spotted a poplar leaf colored bright yellow. Last year, my first winter alone, the electricity was off for days, and the house I bought doesn't have anything but electric baseboard heat. No fireplace, no wood-burning stove. It was scary being stranded, but I'm afraid of those kerosene heaters. I don't know if I can afford a generator, though. Or if I have the strength to pull the rope on the starter, with my bad shoulder. It's been acting arthritic ever since I broke it. It was stupid to try water skiing with Karl and his drunken buddies driving the boat.

"Hey, Caroline." I know the hearty voice before I even turn to see the owner. It's Karl. My heart drops into my stomach. He should be out trying to lure corporate prospects, not roaming around Mercer Mall. Especially not today.

"Hey." We parted on friendly enough terms, but I still feel a little ill at this unexpected encounter.

"What brings you here?" Karl is smiling at me, relaxed, like we're old friends.

"Getting ready for winter." Why did my momma have to teach me to be so polite? I want to say, "Why don't you just go to hell and leave me alone?" Instead, I ask, "How come you're not at work?"

"I met a client for lunch. I was just taking a shortcut back to the car." By way of the power tools, of course.

"Hey, could you stop at the house? I got something I need to give you."

I just blink at him for a time. "Today?"

"Yeah, it won't take long. I'd like you to see what I've done to the house."

"Well--"

"Please." There's that familiar crooked grin.

Curiosity elbows aside good sense. "All right."

What he's done is violate every decorating rule I ever saw in magazines. My beautiful contemporary house is no longer an oasis of soothing, neutral tones. "What do you call that color?" I ask, staring at the dark paint covering the walls of the entry hall and living room.

"Black Cherry," Karl says. "Rich-looking, isn't it?"

We walk into the living room. The brick fireplace is painted an even darker, almost black tone. And then I see it. I step to the lamp and touch the stained-glass shade. "Where did you get that?"

"Nice, isn't it?" Karl says. "It's real Tiffany. I got it in Roanoke." I have to kill him. No jury, at least none with women on it, would send me to prison.

"Come meet the puppy." Karl heads down the hall. I follow, then pause before a large painting hanging on the wall. It's an original P. Buckley Moss that I'd admired in a gallery. Karl turns around. "That wall needed something, didn't it?" Not one female juror would blame me.

He opens the door to the kitchen and a wrinkled, piebald creature comes padding over to me. "This is Rosebud." The puppy, nearly grown, grins at me. When I reach down to pat her, her tongue darts out from what is going to be a massive jaw to lick my nose. "She loves to do that."

"She's sweet." She would have looked cute in my own old living room of taupe, mink brown and eggshell shades. "I always thought you said that with all the traveling you did that you couldn't--"

He cuts me off. "I found out you can get pet sitters to come into your home." Rosebud paddles over to the sliding glass door. "You want to go out, girl?" Karl asks, in a dripping sweet voice that makes me want to throw up. He opens the door and Rosebud tumbles outside. "Come on out," Karl says. "It's nice out here."

I sit in a new redwood chair and notice a few bright red dogwood berries on the deck. The droppings of death. We're in for a bad winter. "When did you get all this?"

"Well, I was having some people over, and . . ." His voice trails off. I probably don't want to know the details. "Hey, you want to see my Wyoming pictures?" Before I can answer he shoots into the house and returns with three fat envelopes. This from a man who wouldn't even go to Hawk's Nest State Park with me to look at the New River Gorge.

"What made you go to Wyoming?"

"One of the guys at work got me started on fly fishing." He passes me a picture of a clear, wide river.

"Can't you fish for trout in West Virginia?" Maybe I'm a little bitter.

"That's not the point." He hands me a shot of a gorgeous mountain range.

I don't understand why he's so eager to show me all about his new life. He was never interested in my opinion before. No use asking him, though. I wouldn't get a real answer, just like I never got an answer to the other questions.

How could you?

Why did you?

Why won't you?

I feel worn out. I need to go home. To my home, the small wooden box with avocado-colored appliances that the seller was happy to let me have. I get up and step back into the kitchen. Rosebud squeezes through the sliding glass door beside me.

Karl is right behind. "Wait, I've got something for you."

Rosebud sits, settling her weight on my foot. I wait. Karl returns with an old green velvet jewelry box. He holds it out like a little boy confident that you'll love the frog he found just for you. He still looks like a little boy, really, with those ruddy cheeks and sandy brows and hair. Rosebud trots over for a sniff.

"What is it?" I don't want anything from him. Except maybe the money he's got in those vehicles and that vacation. I could have a top-of-the-line generator, maybe two, for the price of the dog sitting on my foot.

"It was Gran's. Go on, look at it."

Something of Gran's. My curiosity instructs my hand to take the box and open it. It's that beautiful cameo pin. I admire the oval rim twisted gold and the way the woman's ivory hair is piled in carved curls, secured by a little notched flower. Another blossom rests on the shoulder of her gown. Her profile shows a delicate nose, a gentle eye and a softly smiling mouth. A very elegant piece.

I close the box and try to give it back to him. His brother has three daughters. "One of your nieces ought to have this."

"Those hellions?" Karl shakes his head. "I don't think so."

"What makes you think she'd want me to have this?"

"Well, she left my brother the house and me the contents, so I figure it's my call. Besides, Gran always liked you."

I open the box again and finger the carved surface. It would be nice to have something I can touch that would bring Gran to mind. But this family heirloom ties me to Karl, too.

"Why do you want me to have this?"

"Well." Karl looks down at the floor, the way he always does when I try to get at the root of something. "I don't know, it just reminded me of the things you like, kind of classy and understated." Then he smiles that lopsided grin of his. "Happy anniversary."

I wink away a tear that's trying to form. He has never, ever remembered our anniversary. Every year, I'd set out a card for him at the breakfast table. And every year, he'd grin and say, "You can have yours this evening." He'd show up later with a card and some gift he'd grabbed on his way home from work.

"Speaking of anniversaries and weddings," Karl says, still looking at the floor, "I got something I need to tell you. I'm getting married around Christmas."

The bastard. It's not the notion of his getting married that bothers me. I knew he wouldn't be alone for long. My blood pressure is rising because he's trying to buy my goodwill with a gift of another woman's jewelry.

"Anybody I know?"

Karl continues to examine the floor. "Well, yes, it was one of those things, I hope you can understand, she's just been so great about checking on me--"

"Just tell me who it is." Rosebud looks in alarm at my raised voice.

He will not meet my eyes. "Beverly."

"Bev?" I shout. "You're marrying Bev?" Rosebud struggles to stand and starts barking.

Karl reaches for the dog. "It's all right, girl. Quiet down."

Rosebud stops barking and starts licking his hand. But I'm just getting wound up. To hell with quiet, understated classiness. He's about to get a dose of hurricane-force anger. I'm going to hurl every hurt I've been holding in. He's going to get everything he deserves. And more.

I start to open my mouth, then close it again without speaking. I envision Karl and Bev at the altar. He's going to get everything he deserves. And more. And so is she. Now I understand. The pin, his showing me the details of his new life. He wants my forgiveness, my blessing. He wants to move forward and he thinks I can clear his conscience.

Finally, Karl looks at me, his face braced for whipping. Part of me still wants to vent as much bile as I can. But I might just end up poisoning myself. No, I'm going to give him what he wants, and maybe in the process free myself.

"Congratulations," I say. Rosebud grins happily at us, saliva dripping from her tongue.

I return to the mall and buy a mailing carton, tape and wrapping paper. The paper is pretty, with a pattern of small, pale golden bells against a creamy background. I buy a cream-colored bow to match. I find the perfect card, too. "Congratulations" is printed in gold on ecru paper. Inside, the card simply says, "On Your Special Day."

Back in the Honda, I wrap the cameo and secure it in the box. Let Karl explain it. He's good at explanations.

Inside the card, I write that I hope they can understand that under the circumstances, it's best that we not remain in contact. Then I head for the post office. Stepping out of the car, I notice a crispness in the air that's energizing. The afternoon sun beams at me, casting the world in new clarity. A bittersweet vine already is producing its yellow-orange fruit. One season is ending, another beginning. Change is coming. And so is my fresh start.

The postal clerk weighs the package and gives me the total. "Anything else?" she asks.

"I don't need a thing," I answer.

Junior

Mommy's painting her fingernails. That means we're going to visit an uncle. I hate fingernail polish. It stinks and it makes her fingers look like they're dripping blood. The lipstick comes next. Then she colors her eyes with a powder from a case that says Willow Green.

I hate it when Mommy puts on her going-out face. When I was little, before I started second grade, I'd cry and beg her not to change her face. When we stay home, she makes macaroni and cheese and plays Chinese checkers with me. When we go to an uncle's, she acts like she doesn't hardly know me.

"Hurry up and get ready, Junior," she says. She yanks her brush through her yellow hair, then sprays it with more stinky stuff.

I wonder which uncle we're going to see. It doesn't matter. None of them like me. At first, they get mad when they see me. But Mommy tells them she can't afford a baby-sitter, I won't be any trouble at all, they'll see. I usually go sit in the kitchen with my coloring book and crayons. If I'm good, Mommy will buy me a chocolate milkshake on the way home, even if it is past my bedtime.

Mommy doesn't say a word in the car. Usually, she turns on the radio and sings and asks me if she don't sound just like Wynona. I'd like to ask if I can play the radio, but I'm afraid she'll get mad and slap me. Most times, I'm better off if I just keep quiet. I look out the window at the yellow and red leaves dropping from the trees.

Mommy parks the car and I grab my dinosaur bookbag and follow her into an apartment building. This looks like a nice place. Maybe I'll get lucky. One time, an uncle ordered a pepperoni pizza. Just for me. He was real nice, that UPS guy.

I can tell this is going to be a bad time as soon as the man answers the door. He looks sick. His eyes are red, his face is all stubbly and he kind of smells.

"Hello, Jason," Mommy says.

The man gets a mad look on his face. "What the hell are you doing here?"

"Junior, meet your father."

I feel like somebody just kicked me in the stomach. I didn't know I had a daddy. I thought I just had uncles. The man looks like he just got kicked, too. He stares at me like I'm some kind of weird insect.

"The resemblance is something, isn't it?" Mommy says. "Same coal-black hair, same begging blue eyes."

"You've come looking for more money."

"No, I come looking for you to do right by your son. No reason for you not to, now that Donna's gone."

"Don't." The man's voice sounds like a scary dog growling. "Don't you speak of her."

"Now you listen here." Mommy can sound scary when she wants to. "Don't go acting like I did this all by myself. You ain't no saint, and you know it. I'd like to know how many there's been since me. Or before me, for that matter. I ain't surprised your wife left. I imagine she caught on to your lies just like I did. You ever wonder how I felt, all these years, living every day with a miniature version of you?"

The man raises his hand and I'm afraid he's going to hit Mommy. But she puffs up like an old hissing cat and keeps right on. "All that's beside the point. I'm going to say my piece and then I'm gone. I've got a man willing to marry me, but he don't want kids. I've taken care of Junior all these years, now it's your turn."

She pushes me through the door, and I bump into the man. I turn around and see Mom's face is wet. The Willow Green drips down her cheeks like clown tears. "I deserve a fresh start. You understand, don't you?" I don't know if she's talking to me or the man.

Then she's gone. The man takes off down the stairs after her, hollering. I run after him, crying, "Mommy, wait! Wait!" But she really is gone. I follow the man back into his apartment. I sit down on a sofa and wait for something to happen.

The man flops down in a chair and rubs his hands over his face. I just sit, trying to be as quiet as I can. Finally, the man looks at me and says, "Well, Buddy, we're in a hell of a fix."

I figure I should say something. "Yes, sir."

"I need a drink. Do you need a drink?"

"If you have plenty." I use this answer a lot, to show people I'm not any trouble.

The man laughs. "Oh, yeah. I got plenty." He walks into the kitchen and comes back with two bottles. He gives me a Pepsi and starts drinking his. It's the same brand of beer my mommy drinks.

He seems like he could be a little friendly. I wait for him to empty his bottle, then I say, "Are you really my daddy?"

The man laughs and shrugs his shoulders. "Probably. I need another beer." He goes into the kitchen and comes back with another bottle. "How you set on Pepsi?"

"Fine."

The man looks at me. “You’re a pretty good kid. You might turn out all right if you had decent parents.” He hunkers down in front of me, takes a big gulp out of his bottle. “Too bad your daddy’s a loser and your momma just ran out on you.”

“Mommy didn’t run out. She just wants you to baby-sit me for awhile.” Sometimes Mommy has a hard time getting the uncles to let me hang around.

“Oh, kid.” He grabs me and hugs me to his chest. He starts to cry. “I got left behind, too.” I hold my Pepsi real tight so it doesn’t spill.

He gets up and walks around and around. “Yes, sir, Buddy, we’re in a hell of a fix.” He walks around some more. He turns on the television, real loud, then turns it off again. Next door, music starts thumping. He pounds on the wall. “Turn that damn stereo down!” The music just gets louder. Outside, a dog starts barking. He yanks open a window and yells, “Shut the hell up!” The dog barks even louder. The man jerks around, then grabs a baseball from a shelf. “I’ll knock the yip right out of that damn mutt.” Then he notices me again.

“Don’t worry, Buddy, I ain’t going to do anything.” His voice is regular again. “That’s my trouble, I never do what I say.” He brings the baseball over to me. “See all them signatures? I was on my way, Buddy. I had a hell of an arm. I was leaving Bluefield for bigger things. Then I got hurt. All it takes is one mistake, Buddy, and you’re screwed over for good.” He puts the ball back on the shelf and stares at it awhile. Finally, he says, “I got to get cleaned up.” He just walks off and leaves me sitting there.

Maybe he won’t mind if I color. I take the Pepsi bottle into the kitchen. Then I open my bookbag, and I feel like I just got kicked again. Mommy put clothes in there. And a bunch of papers that look important.

The man is back, clean and shaved. "Come on, Buddy. We're going for a visit." Maybe he's going to find Mommy. I grab my bookbag and run after him.

We don't find Mommy. Instead, I'm sitting in some old lady's kitchen, drinking cocoa. I think she might be one of those grandmas like the kids at school have. She's talking to herself. "I don't have a thing a child would care about. Not one potato chip or cookie. Oh, wait, here." She drags out a box of saltines and a jar of peanut butter. She makes up a whole plate of peanut butter and crackers and sets it on the table in front of me. "There you go."

I take another drink of cocoa, waiting for her to start eating. "Don't you like crackers?" she asks.

"If you have plenty." I have to be careful not to seem like I want too much.

"I fixed all this for you."

"Really?"

"Really. You just take your time. I'll be back." She walks into her living room, and I hear her start to talk to the man. My daddy. I take a cracker and lick the peanut butter before I crunch it. It tastes so good. I eat another. And another. Then I notice the voices are getting louder. I creep over to the doorway, where I can hear every word.

"You want me to do what?" The old lady sounds mad.

"I want you to help me raise the boy, Momma."

"I'm too old to start in on another family. Besides, look how you turned out."

"You taught me to do the right thing, and for once that's what I'm trying to do. But I don't know where to start. You see how he is. The kid's afraid of everything."

They both just sit there. Then the old lady says, "The mother just left?"

"Didn't even hug him good-bye."

I can't help it. I start crying. "I want my mommy." Then I start screaming. "I want my mommy! I want my mommy!"

"Oh my God," my daddy says.

The old lady grabs me and sits down in a rocking chair. "I want my mommy!" I know I might get hit for hollering, but I can't help it. I'm afraid of her. She's got spots and her skin folds up funny. Her hair looks like salt and pepper mixed up. I keep on crying, and she keeps on rocking and saying, "It's all right."

She doesn't have any fake color on her face. Her lap is really warm. And she smells a little like the inside of my bookbag. "It's all right," the old lady says. "You're going to be all right." She takes a tissue from a pocket and wipes my nose.

I look over at my daddy. He's hunched up, his hands over his face. "I can't deal with this," he says.

"Well, you're going to have to," the old lady says quietly. "This little boy needs you." Nobody says anything, and she keeps rocking. She looks like she's thinking real hard. Then, very slowly, she sets me down. "Boys, we got work to do."

I don't know what she's talking about it. She asks my daddy, "Does this child have a coat?"

"Well, uh, I don't guess so," he says.

"Never mind." The old lady goes to a closet and pulls out one of those scratchy sweaters. She buttons it on me, rolling up the sleeves. "Come on."

When we get outside, she tells my daddy to get the rakes out of the garage. When he comes back, she says, "By the time you all get these leaves raked in a pile, I'll have supper ready." I look around her yard. There must be two million leaves. At least.

"Right now?" my daddy asks. He looks at her like she might be crazy.

"You got someplace you'd rather be?"

"No, ma'am."

The old lady looks at me. "You reckon you could work up an appetite for meatloaf and mashed potatoes?" I nod.

"Well, Buddy, this is another fine mess you've got us in," my daddy says to me as the old lady heads inside. I stare at the ground, wondering what I've done wrong now. "Relax," he says. "It's just a joke. Reckon we might as well get started."

"I don't know what to do."

"Watch the master at work."

"Like this?" I drag the rake over the leaves.

"You got it, Buddy."

The pile gets bigger and bigger. Daddy puts the rakes back. The old lady comes out and I wonder what she's going to do with all those leaves.

"Perfect," she says. "You boys did a fine job." She looks at me, waves a hand at the pile and says, "Be my guest."

I don't know what she wants me to do. "Jump," she says. "Jump." I still don't understand. She turns to my daddy. "Maybe you'd better show him."

"Not in my good pants--"

"You two are a real pair," the old lady says. All of a sudden, she throws up her arms and falls on the leaves. "Come on in," she tells me. "I didn't even break a hip." She swishes her arms around, throwing leaves up in the air. "Doesn't this look like fun?"

"I don't want to." I look over at my daddy. He's not doing it.

"What the hell." He flops down on the other side of the pile. He starts laughing and waving at me. "Come on, Buddy. Jump. Don't worry, I'll catch you."

"Jump," the old lady says.

Both of their arms reach for me. They want me. I close my eyes and jump.

Marital Bliss

Roscoe is so good to me. Never an argument in our thirty-five years together. Well, recently he's started harping about buying a recreational vehicle. He's been drooling ever since he went to that RV rodeo at the state fairgrounds. "I spent my whole life in West Virginia," he whines. Roscoe is a good man, but he's always taking notions. Even his body, tall and ropy, seems ready to sway at the whim of a breeze. I'm the steady one, built stout and low to the ground.

"What's wrong with West Virginia?" I ask. I feel snug and protected by the mountains surrounding me. I don't need to see anything else.

"Nothing, but I thought I'd take early retirement from the plant and see something of this country before I get too old." His blue eyes stare past me, toward some old dried-up desert. "I want to feel what it's like to be free, nothing to worry about but the road ahead."

"It sure wouldn't be free. It'd be mighty expensive just buying gasoline."

Roscoe blinks, like he's forgotten all about me. "We could go see the kids." They're a little flighty, too. I don't know why our boy thought he had to go to Oklahoma to find construction work. Our girl sells strange metal sculptures to tourists in Florida.

I get real nervous at the idea of change. "The kids will be in at Christmas. We can't afford an RV," I say, just like I'd told him five years earlier that we couldn't afford a motor boat. A few years before that, it was an in-ground pool. It seems to me that Roscoe's never satisfied, but he argues that I'm still living in the Depression. There's some truth to that. I've never forgotten me and my brothers and sisters crying and hanging on to Mommy and Daddy at that foreclosure sale. Never forgotten what it's like to have nothing to call my own.

Roscoe drags a handkerchief out of his pocket and wipes his nose. "You better get that prescription filled," I remind him.

"My allergies might not bother me so much out West."

"I don't know about that," I say. "But I know we can't afford for you to take early retirement." I want to make sure there's enough to take care of us in our old age. I'm not counting on my children's charity. I've always planned ahead. I'm the one who insisted on buying big life insurance policies while the children were still in school. Roscoe was wanting a new truck at the time, but I made him see that it was important to provide for his family. I had him take out one on me, too, because it would be expensive to bring someone in to cook and care for the children.

"Pleasure just ain't in your vocabulary, is it, Dotty?" I wouldn't exactly call that an argument, but his words did hurt my feelings. Somebody's got to be responsible. Luckily for me, his mother always backs me up. "Roscoe," she tells him, "You just quit your foolishness and be thankful you got such a good helpmate." Roscoe never contradicts his mother.

And it's not like I'm cheap. The children never wanted for anything, and we have a nice brick ranch that's almost paid off. Of course, Roscoe works hard, driving to

Covington every day to the mill. I make a little extra money quilting, but not much. My stitches are small and consistent, but people just don't want to pay for the time that goes into handiwork.

I think he's finally dropped the subject of RVs. I can tell Roscoe is sorry for acting so selfish, because he's been extra considerate. He insists on getting my Mercury Marquis serviced before me and my cousin Wanda go to Waynesboro to the factory outlet stores for some early Christmas shopping. Since Wanda lives in Princeton, I'd like her to spend the night, but she gets on Roscoe's nerves.

Wanda dressed for the morning chill, wearing a sweatshirt painted with pumpkins. I'm sure her friend Viola made it for her. Both of us are wearing white tennis shoes because we know we're going to do a lot of walking. Wanda ought to use a cane, too, but she refuses to act her age. She wanted to take her car, but she's a terrible driver. At fifty-eight, I might not have the sharpest reflexes, but Wanda is a menace. She just pulls out in front of traffic. Says she can't wait forever.

We pass into Virginia and get as far as Clifton Forge before trouble hits. "What's that racket?" Wanda asks.

"I don't know." A sort of slapping sound is coming from the driver's side. "Maybe I ran over something and punctured a tire." I drive off the exit and find a gas station with a garage bay. Wanda stumbles off to find a restroom. Her back wouldn't be so crooked if she took calcium, but there's no use saying anything to her. She claims she's bent over from all her years as a nurse. But I guess she gets around as good as the next person.

"I reckon I need a new tire," I tell the mechanic, who is about my age. The embroidered patch on his blue-and-white striped shirt reads, "Possum." The stripes are muted by a grayish hue. I feel sorry for the woman who's tried to wash away all that oil and grease.

"I can sell you a tire, but we'd better make sure that's the problem," Possum says.

Wanda returns. "Your toilet's locked and I'm about to wet my pants." Wanda doesn't care what she says.

"Key's hanging beside the cash register," Possum tells her, pointing. He hunkers beside the front left tire. "You say the sound come from here?"

"That's right." Wanda hobbles by, carrying a key hanging from a chunk of wood carved in the shape of a locomotive.

"Just for the heck of it, I'm going to check your lug nuts." I watch as Possum tightens one by hand. "That ain't good," he says in a quiet voice.

I reach out to try one of the nuts and just about pass out when it twirls in my hand. Possum checks the rest. Every one of them as loose as my cousin Ivy.

"Ma'am, you were lucky you made it here." Possum's face is sober. "That wheel could have come off just any time. If you'd been going highway speed . . ." He didn't have to finish the sentence.

"How could that be? My husband just had my car serviced." Roscoe is going to be so mad.

"I don't know, maybe whoever worked on it got in a hurry and just forgot that last wheel. You hold on and I'll get my wrench and torque those nuts for you."

"How much will that cost?" I ask, wondering if I should call Roscoe.

"I'm not going to charge you anything. It'll only take me five minutes." I am constantly surprised at how nice people can be.

The rest of the trip goes fine. Nobody can say I'm cheap when it comes to Christmas. I remember the first

Christmas I found an orange in my stocking when I was a little girl. I'd never seen an orange before, and I just took a big bite out of it. I thought it was delicious, rind and all. I like to make sure everyone has a good Christmas. At the Van Heusen store, I buy Roscoe some nice shirts. Wanda picks up several packages of panties for herself at the Hanes outlet. We just go crazy at the Corning outlet store. You just can't beat Corning for cookware. Wanda is fingering some casserole dishes. I'm going to buy them for her and tell her they're for Ivy.

Roscoe is obsessed about vehicle maintenance now. "I cussed that mechanic but good," he tells me. He's insisting that me and Wanda take his Blazer to the Southern Living cooking show in Beckley. I tell him my Mercury is fine. I don't want to drive his Blazer with that embarrassing bumper sticker: "If you don't like my driving, get off the sidewalk."

"It sits up higher and you can see around those tractor trailers better," he says, his eyes running from the autumn pollen. He goes into the kitchen and gets his allergy pills and grapefruit juice to wash them down. I need to remember to pick up some more juice on the way home.

It's terribly foggy. We haven't even left Lewisburg and I've almost rear-ended two cars on U.S. 219. "Dotty, what's wrong with you today?" Wanda snaps.

"I don't know. I guess I'm not judging distance very good in this vehicle. Maybe it's just the fog." Sitting at the traffic light, I take a couple of deep breaths and pat my hair. I always love that polished feel of a fresh shampoo and set.

"Maybe the brakes are bad," Wanda says. "Maybe we ought to turn around and get my car."

"No, it can't be the brakes. Roscoe said it's just been serviced." I drive on up the ramp to the interstate.

"What's that chirping sound?"

"I don't know. Maybe it's the ABS."

"What's ABC?" Wanda doesn't even try to keep up with current events. But she cooks from scratch the fluffiest biscuits, and a butterscotch pie that makes you glad for every one of your taste buds.

"Anti-lock Braking System," I say. "I sure hope this fog lifts soon." The haze is even denser on the interstate, so thick you can hardly make out the red and yellow leaves on the maples and poplars. If I was sitting on my porch, with a cup of coffee, I might think it was right pretty, a misty curtain waiting to reveal the day's colors. Better than a Branson show. I do dread the time when the trees lose their leaves. It seems to me each winter is colder than the last.

"What's that?" Wanda digs in her purse, hands me a Certs and pops one in her mouth. She would give me the lint-covered one on top. Then she hauls out a comb and drags it through her sparse white hair.

"According to Roscoe, it means you don't pump your brakes in an emergency. All you got to do is stomp real hard."

"Stomp!" Wanda hollers, just as I see red brake lights glowing right in front of me. I stomp. Nothing. Not even the slightest bit of resistance. I swerve onto the shoulder and just kept riding, trying to scrub off speed. I grew up on one-lane West Virginia roads where you have to drop two wheels off to the right when you meet a vehicle. I know better than to jerk the steering wheel right back on the highway. Finally, we reach a hill and the Blazer stops.

"Lord have mercy!" Wanda's eyes bulge from their sockets. She burrows deep in her purse and brings out a handkerchief to mop her face.

"That ABS sure didn't work very good, did it?" I say, trying to stay calm for Wanda's sake.

"ABC, hell." Wanda wipes her forehead. "This thing don't have brakes at all."

I squeeze the accelerator pedal just a tad and creep along the shoulder to the next exit. I spot a gas station and drive up to the garage bay.

"Is your toilet locked?" Wanda asks.

The young man steps over to the cash register and grabs a board shaped like the state of West Virginia. "Here you go." He walks back into the bay, pulls a wheel and brings the brake pads for me to inspect. "Lady, you were coasting on luck. Look, you didn't have any pad left at all." They look as if they'd been filed down.

"That can't be," I say. "My husband is very careful about vehicle maintenance."

"Well, you don't have brakes now," he says. "You want me to see if I can get new pads?"

The mechanic's curly hair is pretty shaggy, and he's wearing an earring. But he seems like a nice young man in his clean uniform. "I guess you'd better." So much for the cooking show. Wanda stumps back inside the station to hang up the key, several squares of toilet paper trailing behind one shoe.

Might as well stop at the super Wal-Mart for a few items. Eggs, milk, bread. Oh, and juice. "I don't drink that stuff," Wanda says. "I read that it can interfere with your medicine."

"That must be for people with stomach problems," I say, grabbing a jar from the refrigerator case. "Roscoe loves grapefruit juice." Wanda might have been a nurse, but I know for a fact that she takes all her pills in the morning so she won't have to fool with them the rest of the day.

We walk into the house to find Roscoe sitting at the kitchen table, a bunch of paperwork spread before him. I can't believe it -- he's mooning over those RV brochures again.

Roscoe gulps, like I'm the last person he expects to see coming through that door. He sweeps those brochures into his lap, his face burning. "Hey," he says.

"Hey."

Roscoe stands up so fast, he tips his chair over and the papers flutter to the floor. I've never seen him act so nervous. He straightens the chair and starts gathering the papers. "I was just going to throw all this stuff out," he babbles. "No use keeping it." The phone rings and he jumps, banging his head on the table. "Dammit to hell," he yelps.

"You cut your forehead," Wanda says. "You better take care of that."

I pick up the phone. "Hello? No, he can't come to the phone. Can I take a message?"

I'm pretty upset by the time Roscoe comes out of the bathroom with a bandage on his head. But I have never raised my voice in our 35 years of marriage. "That was some salesman saying he had those RV prices you wanted."

Roscoe's cheeks turn the shade of a ripe Best Boy tomato. "I swear, I wonder how people that incompetent stay in business," he says. "I left a message for him not to call anymore."

"Speaking of incompetent, you'll never guess what happened to me and Wanda today," I say. I forget all about recreational vehicles when I see the concern on Roscoe's face, which is growing redder. "You don't look too good. Maybe you ought to take some of your allergy medicine."

Roscoe rummages in a cabinet for his pills, and I fill an iced-tea glass with grapefruit juice. Roscoe gulps his down so fast that I pour him another glass. He chugs that one, too.

I still feel bad about what happened. For once, Wanda knew what she was talking about. She called the rescue squad when we saw Roscoe turning the color of Elmer's glue, but it was too late. The doctor explained about how the combination of the allergy medicine and so much grapefruit juice caused some enzyme in the intestinal wall to drop and the drug level to increase, which made Roscoe's blood pressure fall so fast that he went into shock. All I really understood was that he was gone.

Because of that insurance policy, Roscoe is still taking care of me, bless his heart.

I miss him so much. This old house is too big and lonesome without him. The squirrels outside my bedroom window are racing around, gathering food for the winter to come. I woke up this morning to find a light layer of white crusting the ground.

I just can't stay here. My daughter's been begging me to come live near her, and I'm going to do it. She's found a little place that she says I'll love. Wanda says I'm crazy, and I can hardly believe I'm making such a drastic change.

I have to make sure Roscoe is all right before I leave. I find myself driving out to the cemetery and standing by his monument, a beautiful big marble slab carved with a drawing of a deer standing in woods, a proud buck gazing toward heaven. Wanda squawked at the money I spent, but I thought Roscoe deserved a nice stone. He was always so good to me. Never an argument in our thirty-five years together. Not many couples can say that.

I squat to brush the snow from the arrangement I bought. It's a nice, sturdy plastic wreath covered with yellow roses. I never foresaw a time when we wouldn't be together. The sky spits a few flakes of snow, which I wipe from the marble. I find myself yanking the gloves off my hands, not caring if they do get chapped. I press one palm against the inscription of Roscoe's name, the other right beside it. I had my name and birthdate engraved, too. It comforts me to know I'm going to lie beside him again some day. My fingers trace the epitaph and I silently mouth the words: "Beloved Husband and Father, Constant and Faithful, Awaiting the Day of Joyful Reunion."

Delivery

If JoAnn doesn't hurry up and make up her mind, I'm going to kill her.

It's not like the three of us haven't met at Cracker Barrel every third Thursday of the month since the damned place opened. Excuse my language, but this place is always packed, standing as it does at the intersection of the West Virginia Turnpike and Interstate 77 in Princeton. I'd just as soon go to Shoney's, where I could finish up with some strawberry pie. But Viola says she's got to have that Cracker Barrel coffee. So we stand in line and stare at the tourists wandering around the gift shop. Then JoAnn acts like she's never seen the menu before.

"Excuse me," she asks the waiter, a good-looking boy with two stars on his apron. Probably one of those Concord College students. "What ingredients do you use to marinate the chicken tenders?"

"I don't know, ma'am, but they sure are good," he says.

"Well, I can't eat just anything. I'm sensitive to certain things." Sensitive, my ass. I've seen her loading Little Debbie Snack Cakes in her grocery cart. JoAnn stretches her lips back from her false teeth in what she thinks is a fetching smile. She always was a flirt.

"Do you want me to go ask the kitchen?" he asks politely, but I see him glancing around nervously at other tables waiting for coffee refills and checks.

"For God's sake, JoAnn, just go ahead and order the damned chicken tenders," I say. "I'll have the meatloaf special. What do you want besides coffee, Viola?"

"That meatloaf sounds good to me, too," Viola says, and the boy speeds off. Viola's not all that picky, except she will insist on a good cup of coffee. Mostly, she's a very comfortable person to be around. Today she's wearing one of those cute sweatshirts with a collar. She painted the cardinal on there herself. I'm wearing one she made me last Christmas. It covers an old woman's fallen bosom and flabby stomach very well.

"Well." JoAnn pats the hair she just had shampooed and set into swirls and curlicues. "You are so impatient, Wanda." JoAnn brushes a speck of napkin lint from her burgundy pant suit. She lives across the state line in Rich Creek, and she always dresses up like she's Virginian gentry. She's as slim as the day she married, although I know for a fact that she still seasons her beans with pork, no matter what she says. That's probably what killed her husband. I also know for a fact that she watches two soap operas every day, although she'd deny it even to the preacher.

I'm surprised she doesn't get a dye job. The hair on all three of us is white as rice. Viola's perm is starting to look shaggy, but it curls real nice around her sweet face. I'm afraid I look a little wild. I get so aggravated sitting around and waiting in the beauty shop that I usually just chop my own hair at home.

The waiter returns with three coffees. JoAnn and Viola both have great-grandchildren his age. I wish I had children and grandchildren. I guess I was barren. Of course, Chester could have been shooting blanks. We just accepted it as God's will. Didn't have the money to see about it, anyway. And JoAnn's right. I'm so impatient. I probably would have been a terrible mother. Back when we were all TB nurses in Beckley, I'd get nervous about everything that had to be done. More than a few times, I admit, instead of gently running the breathing tube through the nose, sometimes I'd get in a hurry and end up ramming it all the way down the throat. I sure as hell hope I don't wind up being nursed by a version of me someday.

After more than eight decades, it seems like all of us are falling apart. I doubt if any of us should drive. JoAnn can't turn her neck, so she just eases on out into traffic and hopes for the best. Viola seems to be shrinking and I wonder if she can even see over the steering wheel. I don't judge distances very well anymore.

The boy slides our plates in front of us and we dig in. "Guess what I did today?" I ask, but I can't wait for an answer. "I stopped by the funeral home today and made my arrangements." I describe every single detail, except the price. That's my business.

Viola looks distressed. "Oh, no, Wanda, don't even think about such things." It doesn't take much to upset Viola ever since her husband got prostate cancer.

"Why not?" I fork a piece of meatloaf. "It's not like I have children to take care of things. Besides, I'll rest better knowing what's what."

JoAnn doesn't look up from cutting a piece of chicken tender. "You won't even know what's what."

I wink at Viola. "You might be surprised. I plan on coming back and checking on things."

JoAnn finishes thoroughly chewing a piece of chicken, then says, "I reckon you will at least have a viewing first."

Those mashed potatoes sure are delicious. "Nope. Just a little memorial service with my urn."

"Wanda, you've got to have a viewing. How are folks supposed to tell you good-bye?" Viola is beginning to act genuinely upset. She's shredding her biscuit instead of eating it.

JoAnn pats Viola's hand. "Don't worry. We'll have a viewing if that's what you want. Wanda won't have anything to say about it."

Suddenly my cinnamon apples don't taste so good. I shake my fork at JoAnn. "Now you just hold on a minute. This is my funeral. You try putting me on display and I swear I'll reach up out of the casket and grab your scrawny neck."

I hear a sort of choking sound and I see the boy standing there with a coffee pot. His face grows redder and redder as he pours refills for us and leaves the checks. He'd better get his blood pressure checked.

"Well," JoAnn says. "You don't have to act so mean about it."

"Why don't you want a viewing?" Viola asks. She's pushing her meat loaf around her plate.

"For one thing, I don't care to have people holding drooling babies over my face. For another, I don't want to be fancied up like some doll. Lastly, I don't want some man touching my private parts."

"Wanda!" Both of them squawk at that.

"That's how I feel." I've got too many miles on me to worry about holding my tongue.

JoAnn looks at her watch. All of us still wear watches with second hands, like we might be called back into nursing duty. "I've got to get back."

"What's your hurry?" I know she's wanting to watch her shows.

"I've just got things to do."

I shoot out of the parking lot first. I can't stand to get behind that slowpoke Viola. She just creeps along, afraid she might squash a squirrel.

A horn blows and then I see a big old brown UPS truck whipping around to the left of me. Oops. I reckon I pulled out in front of him. I wave and smile at the fellow to show him I didn't do it on purpose. Of course, he was probably going too fast, anyway. But he looked like a nice boy.

I calm down as my car turns on to the side road that leads to my house. I love this little lane, especially this time of year, when the maples burn red and yellow. If it was just a little warmer, I'd roll down my window and listen to the sound of the creek that flows beside to the road. I was baptized in that water.

Suddenly, right in front of me a deer seems to jump straight up from the earth. "Sweet Jesus!" I holler and wrench the steering wheel. I miss the deer, but I've run across the other lane, clear off the pavement. I jerk the wheel again to get back on the road. Now I can't straighten the damn car. Dear God, I'm headed straight for the creek.

It's so strange how everything happens so quickly, yet I feel suspended in time. This is it. I'm about to meet my maker. Then the car comes to a stop and I seem to be alive. I take my pulse just to be sure. I sure am glad to still be here. I'd hate for JoAnn and Viola to find out I went off this morning and left dishes in the sink.

All right, I'll just sit here and wait until help comes.

Cold water covers my feet and starts inching up to my ankles. I realize that folks won't start getting off work for hours. It looks like I'll either drown or die of exposure. Ouch. There goes that angina. I fumble around for my purse and grab a pill. There. That's better. I always wondered what it must have been like for that poor little girl riding with that Kennedy boy.

Maybe I shouldn't have taken that pill. If this is my time, I'd just as soon get it over with. I wished now I'd stopped and got a new *Enquirer*. At least I'd have something to read. I don't know if I could concentrate, though. My head hurts a little. Might have bumped my head on the steering wheel.

The water works its way up my calves. I'm starting to feel so cold. Well, maybe it won't be long now. I lean back and close my eyes and try to think grateful thoughts for the life I was given. But I wish I could have learned to master my temper and tongue. I kind of wish I'd had children, but now it makes me tired just to think of trying to raise a family. Still, if only I could have had just one day with a little grandchild. I'd have bought him a big old ice cream cone. I bet he would have picked chocolate.

Maybe things work out the way they're supposed to. Maybe it was meant for me to make my funeral arrangements today. Then I start thinking about JoAnn's smart remark, "Wanda won't have anything to say about it." She wouldn't have the nerve to go against my directions. Not after I threatened her. Then again, she just might, for pure spite. And especially if Viola starts crying about seeing me one last time. I just hate the idea of people standing around, saying, "Doesn't she look good?"

The hell with that. I grab the door handle and push. To my surprise, it opens. I don't know why I didn't even try it before. I guess I just assumed I'd be trapped, like that girl. My feet don't want to work, though. I grab hold of the door frame and pull myself forward, grunting and groaning.

Now I'm worse off than I was before. I'm halfway out of the car, but my feet don't want to move. I reckon I can crawl. I grab on to one rock, then another, keeping my head out of the water. Just when I think I'm going to have to give up, I make it to the bank and flop down. Whew.

I hear a deep loud rumbling. Must be the UPS truck heading to the Bennetts about a mile down the road. I swear I wonder what in the world those people could be needing delivered all the time. The truck pulls over and the driver runs toward me. I believe it's the same fellow that almost ran over me. Those UPS boys always look so neat and clean.

"Ma'am, Ma'am," he hollers at me. "Are you hurt?"

"Well, I ain't deaf," I tell him. "But I am a mite wet."

Next thing I know he's got me situated in his truck. "I'd better get you straight to the hospital."

"Take me on home. I just need some dry clothes and I'll be all right."

"Ma'am, you really ought to see a doctor."

"I live just a couple of miles down the road," I tell him. "You help me in my house and then I'll see about a doctor and calling Triple A. Besides, I know you boys got a schedule to keep."

He looks doubtful, then grins and says, "You're just like my grandma. She was full of spit and vinegar, too."

I smile back at him, even if he is driving fast enough to rearrange my intestines. I feel reckless, too. "What's your name?"

"William." Damn it to hell. He would have to hit that particular pothole.

"Do you like ice cream, Billy?"

He looks at me like I'm a crazy old woman, then grins again. "Sure."

"What's your favorite flavor?"

"Chocolate, ma'am."

It just so happens I've got a box of fudge ripple in my freezer. I don't care if he does have a schedule. I'm going to feed this boy a dish of ice cream.

Picasso's Cat

I never knew Christmas could be so lonesome. All the guys at the print shop are itching to find out whether they're going to get the Craftsmen tools they've been drooling over in Mercer Mall. Poor Marvin thinks he's going to find a big, red, rolling tool chest under the tree. With ball bearing drawer slides. Yeah, right.

I'm just waiting to find out what else I'm going to lose. Already lost my wife. She complained for two years that I wouldn't communicate. I never could understand what she wanted from me, so I'd stare at the television, hoping her issue of the month would blow itself out like a quick thunderstorm. By the time I figured out I'd better find some way to talk to her, she was on her way to Roanoke.

And ever since the shop lost its biggest account, the boss has been eyeballing me like a fishing boat he can't afford to keep up. Not much to show for my first quarter of a century, except a fairly decent car, and I'm going to have to seriously consider refinancing if I have any hope of keeping it.

Still, this has been a pretty good morning, considering everything. I'm just sitting at my computer, pointing and clicking up a storm with my mouse. I don't know why so many people are afraid of art. It's nothing in the world more than shapes and shadows. Two years at the community college and you got yourself the title of graphics designer.

This particular little job I'm working on is a logo for a writer. That woman drove me crazy yesterday, describing all these moods and impressions she wanted to convey symbolically on her stationery. I pushed my wire-rims back to the bridge of my nose and said, "Yes, ma'am. I understand completely." Actually, I'd drifted away to wondering whether the Bengals had any hope of making the playoffs.

I don't intend to be rude. I just don't know what to say. I'll wrap the writer's name in a script font around a real nice quill and inkpot. Suddenly, I hear this god-awful shriek. For a second, I figure Marvin caught his hand in the press again. Then I realize the sound is coming from the other side of the door. I jump up and jerk it open to find a cat glaring at me like I have really screwed up big time. Now, a ginger tabby can be a pretty sight, but this specimen looks like he's gone through the spin cycle a few too many times. Scars track across his face. One ear appears to be thoroughly chewed. His tail crooks like a proofreader's mark.

The critter jerks his head toward the garbage bin, then yowls again. "This ain't no restaurant," I tell him, ready to slam the door.

He slips through before I can shut it. Just as I'm thinking about grabbing him and pitching him outside, he starts rubbing around my legs. "Aw, for God's sake."

He's so skinny, he could almost slide under the door. I reach in my desk drawer where I keep a handy supply of Slim Jims. He tears into that stick of beef jerky like it's the best stuff he ever tasted. Then he yowls again, showing me his fangs, like this will show me who's in charge. I give him another Slim Jim. And another.

Just then my boss walks in, a piece of paper clutched in his hand. "What the hell's going on back here, Buddy?" He never calls me by my name, Randall.

"Well, J.T., I heard this noise --"

"I see you don't have enough work to keep you busy." I open my mouth to explain, but I don't get the chance. "I can fix that in a hurry. About time you start pulling your weight around here."

That's not fair. I should tell him that I never miss a customer deadline and that nobody has ever complained about the quality of my work. Instead, I start to sweat and say, "What -- what do you mean?"

"I mean you're going to spend your afternoons making sales. I want you to push your design background. Throw around some fancy art words. Make us stand out from the competition."

The idea of asking people for business is so far beyond me that I think my heart might just quit on me. I can't say that, though. "But -- how am I supposed to get all my other work done?"

For just a minute, J.T. drops his drill sergeant routine. He looks as weary as an old dog crawling off to die. "Buddy, if we don't build our customer base, it won't matter." Then he shrugs off the moment and hands me a list of business. "Here, I was just working on some prospects. Might as well get started." He glowers at the cat. "Drop that fleabag at the shelter on your way out." The cat narrows his eyes and growls at J.T.

Nobody sasses J.T. and gets away with it. "Cat, how would you like to take a cruise in a sack full of rocks?"

I know he'd make good on the threat. I don't give a damn about this cat, but the creature at least deserves a quick end. I grab some design samples and giveaway calendars and tell J.T., "I'm already on my way out. I'll get rid of the cat."

The fleabag trots after me, no doubt hoping for another helping of beef jerky. He hops right in the car and settles in the passenger seat, twitching his ears at the sound of the electric locks. I carry my laptop computer with me sometimes, so I try to stay in the habit of locking the doors.

"Don't even think this is some rescue mission," I tell him. "Thanks to you, my boss thinks I'm about as valuable as a book of clip art." The cat cocks his head at me, then slinks over to my lap and makes himself at home, shedding orange hair on my pants. By the time I pull into the parking lot of the animal shelter, he's purring like the happiest creature in the world.

"Well, cat, this is where you and me part company," I tell him as I turn off the ignition. He stands up, arches his back and opens his mouth wide to reveal those mighty fangs. I figure he's about to shred me. But all he does is yawn and relax back into his regular cock-eyed posture. Then the damned thing touches his nose to mine and purrs. Suddenly, I feel kind of like a daddy.

"For crying out loud." I push him away.

But I can't bring myself to open the door. Instead, I start the car and head straight to the drive-through at the Dairy Queen and order us some lunch. "One hamburger basket, one large coffee, one foot-long hot dog, no bun and a carton of milk." The cat's head bobs with the motion of the electric window.

There's a little patch of grass that passes for a park in this town. The cat and I have the picnic tables all to ourselves on this December day. I welcome the brisk air and the quiet. Maybe I can settle down and find the courage to make that first call.

Gnawing my hamburger, I try to distract myself by thinking up a name for this critter gulping down a hot dog right off the top of the table. Maybe I'll name him after a famous artist. He looks kind of like a Picasso version of a cat, especially with that weird bent tail. That man couldn't draw a lick. I don't think he was quite right in the head.

"Hey, Picky." He stops eating long enough to look at me and respond with that screech that passes for a meow. I open the carton and fold the flaps so he can get at the milk. Picky slurps happily. A couple of hours ago, his gut hurt from emptiness. Now mine aches with fear.

I'm going to have to face that first door sooner or later. "Come on, Picky." He trots right behind me and jumps in the car as soon as I open the door. His ears twitch again when I hit the electric locks. I click the locks a couple of more times just for entertainment.

First stop, Franklin's Automotive Service. As soon as I pull up, I understand why they named this activity cold calling. My insides, especially where I should have some guts, feel like sharp ice crystals. I turn the key to the accessory position to keep the heater going for Picky. Something tells me I won't be gone long enough to worry about draining the battery. Picky watches my departure from the passenger seat, washing lunch from his whiskers.

Gripping my samples, I get out of the car and walk stiff-legged into the garage, where I stammer my introduction to Franklin. He takes less than a minute to explain very clearly that he doesn't need any of what I'm selling. Franklin possesses the kind of physical stature that doesn't invite argument. I drag myself back to the car.

I can't get in. I yank on the handle a dozen times before my brain finally registers the information that the door seemed to be locked. I peer inside. Squinting back at me is Picky, standing in my seat, looking very proud of himself. One paw rests precisely on the lock position of the side control panel.

"Why, you little--" And then I stop myself. Franklin's watching me from the plate glass door of his front door, no doubt wondering why I'm still on the lot. In a low, pleasant tone that I hope will somehow penetrate that small skull, I say, "Come on, Picky, move over this way." I snap my fingers over the button that would unlock the door. Picky raises his other paw and playfully bats at my fingers.

I spend several embarrassing minutes snapping my fingers, waving my hands and finally flat out pleading with that stupid cat to inch over. Customers give me curious looks as they pass in and out of the garage. A UPS driver frowns at me as he walks by with a package. "Look at that cute kitty," says an older lady with white curly hair. I hear the younger and equally curly version of the woman hissing, "Come on, Mom. This guy's weird."

"Is there a problem?" Franklin appears at my side.

"Well, sir, it seems I locked my car with the keys inside--"

But Franklin can't miss Picky's scraggly face plastered against the glass. He moves a little closer to the window, then busts out laughing. "Hey, y'all, come here!" he hollers to his mechanics.

Franklin's employees gladly leave their work bays to gather around. Customers are checking out the show, too. "Look, here," Franklin sputters, wiping his eyes, "This guy's cat locked him out of his car!" You could have heard the hee-hawing all the way to the next county.

Picky's so scared by all that noise that now he's frozen in place. Cats do that. I guess they figure that if they pretend they're not there, the problem will go away.

As if all this wasn't enough bad enough, I see I'm going to have to ask these jackasses for help. Trying to sound casual, I say, "You reckon you fellows could get this unlocked?"

Franklin wipes his eyes again, then motions to a hulk of a man in a blue work shirt and pants. He looks a lot like the guy who used to beat me up after gym class in high school.

"There you go, Buddy." The door stands miraculously open. People start drifting away. I just stare at the dumb animal now cowering on the floorboard. Then a hand claps my back so hard, I stumble.

"Son, you just can't win for losing, can you?" Franklin says in sympathy.

"That's just about right, sir," I say, staring at Picky and thinking about how I had fed my own destruction.

Franklin pulls his wallet out of his pocket and takes out a business card. "Tell you what. I could use some more cards. You give me a decent price and do a good job, and maybe we'll talk invoices."

I can't believe it. I thank Franklin and scramble for the car before he can change his mind. Picky purrs from the passenger seat, looking very pleased with himself. "You rascal," I say to him. "I don't know whether to wring your neck or give you a commission."

Next stop, a small medical supply company. I'm not about to leave the keys in the car this time. Picky will just have to rough it. The moment I step into the foyer, complimentary calendar extended, the office manager says, "I know you, you're the guy with the cat! Me and Janice just got back from picking up my truck, and between you and me, I still don't think I needed a new master cylinder." I'm already backing up when she hollers, "Hey, Janice, the guy with the cat's here!" Before I can make it to the door, she says, "Hold on just a second, we've been thinking about adding color to our stationery. Make it look more professional. Can you do that?"

"Yes ma'am, I sure can." I creep forward and give her the calendar.

She looks at the name of my company and says, "I went to grade school with J.T. Know what the initials stand for?" I shake my head. "Jeremiah Thessalonians. His parents wanted to name him after the Old and New Testaments! Can you imagine? Boy, did we tease him."

Half an hour later, I leave with a sizable order in my hand. I find Picky snoozing in my seat.

The rest of the afternoon goes great. Some people even call the office looking to do business with "that guy with the cat." J.T. nearly dropped his dentures when I called him, "Jeremiah," but he's thrilled with the bottom line.

Picky is thrilled, too, when I take him through the drive-through of Long John Silver's for supper. As we wait for our three-piece fish dinners, Picky snuggles up to me and lays one of those embarrassing nose rubs on me.

"For crying out loud," I say.

"Isn't that sweet?" About the prettiest redhead I've ever seen leans out the takeout window. "I just love cats." One of her eyes is green. The other is brown. All of a sudden, this seems so much better than two of the same color.

I squint at her name tag. I can see myself opening Christmas presents with Anita. Her hair would look so pretty with a dark green cedar tree as backdrop. I try to think of something to say to her. I've never asked anybody out. My ex sort of chose me for her boyfriend when we were high school seniors. Just then, Picky pokes his head out the window and yowls at her. Then he shows her his fangs.

"He is so cute!" Anita leans even further out the window. "I bet you just got him at the shelter, didn't you?"

"Well--"

"I think that is so wonderful. It really says something about you as a person." A car rolls up behind me and she retreats back inside the window to take the order.

Picky stares at me with intent focus. I start to sweat.

"Here you go." Anita hands me a bag of food and change.

"Anita--"

"Yes?" Her smile is gentle and encouraging.

"Would--would you like to go out sometime?" I think I'm going to be too sick to eat.

She turns away. "Sorry."

My gut twists and I prepare to drive off. She waves at me to stay. "Ma'am, we're not running that special now." She's talking into her headset microphone. "I'll give you a few minutes to look at the menu."

Anita turns back to me. "Tell you what. I'm off Saturday. Let's meet at the mall at noon and get a couple of those paper angels off that big Christmas tree. Wouldn't it be fun buying toys for some disadvantaged kids?"

"Well--sure." Reading the phone book with her would be fun.

"Maybe we'll find a catnip mouse for your little friend, too." She winks at Picky. "Well, I'd better get back to work. I'll meet you by the Sears entrance." She slides the glass window shut. I drive off with a big grin on my face, while Picky sniffs the bag with great interest. Saturday, I'm going to buy him a collar. With a jingle bell.

The Bridge

. . . This is a world of sweets and sours . . .
-- Edgar Allan Poe, "Israfel," 1831

"Don't come near me. I'll jump!" As if I care about some stupid girl prancing at the edge of the bridge like a drunken majorette.

"Go ahead," I say. "You're standing in my spot, anyway." Damn, I'm freezing. Back in my room, staring at an old baseball glove and trying to work out a new poem, New Year's Eve seemed like perfect timing. And the river seemed the perfect place, especially with that line from Poe rattling around in my mind. *Resignedly beneath the sky the melancholy waters lie*. Poe never really knew his dad, either.

Now, though, that West Virginia wind whips right through my jeans and coat. This state is so depressing in the winter. Nothing but a bunch of naked trees shivering through one storm after another. Too bad my dad never invited me to come live with him in South Carolina. Or wherever he is now. He'll probably go golfing tomorrow. In his shirt sleeves.

The girl squints at me, like I'm crazy. If she's looking for somebody to talk her down, she'd better look somewhere else. "What do you mean, I'm in your spot?"

"That's where I'm going to jump. Exactly at midnight." Old year passes into the new, I pass from one dimension to another. There's a full moon, too. *Mid-time of night; and stars, in their orbits, shone pale, thro' the light of the brighter, cold moon.* Heavy-duty symbolism. *Herself in the heavens, her beam on the waves. I gazed awhile on her cold smile; too cold -- too cold for me.* "You got about twenty minutes to finish your business."

She looks like she's about my age, maybe a junior or a senior. Her long blonde hair shines white in the moonlight. "Are you nuts? You can't save places for suicide like -- like you're saving a seat for somebody on the bus."

This is all I need, a hysterical female like my mom. "I'm just saying I'd appreciate it if you'd be out of my way by midnight."

"Maybe I'm waiting until midnight," she says, tossing her hair the way pretty girls do to get attention. They're usually not wanting my attention, though. I look like the kind of guy who might make a fortune in computers one day. Or be remembered as the loner when the television crews go looking for the story behind the sniper attack.

"Why don't you just go on home? You don't seem all that depressed to me." It's cold as hell out here. I pull my black knit cap below my ears. Mom's best friend, a stylist on training wheels, just about scalped me the last time she cut my hair.

"Well, I am." Another hair toss.

I turn away and walk back to my car. Maybe if I ignore her, she'll get bored and leave. I crank the engine of my AMC Pacer, the best ride I can afford working after school and weekends at the Dairy Queen. Nothing. Again. Nothing. Piece of -- there it goes. I turn on the heater at full blast. No sense being uncomfortable. That's my dad's motto, anyway. I reach for the cracked dash and reposition the envelope, just to make sure it's visible.

In a few minutes, the door opens and the girl climbs in. "Do you mind? It's freezing out there." She blows on her bare hands. She's got some guy's chunky class ring wrapped in yarn to fit her thin finger. That ski jacket didn't come from Wal-Mart.

"You walked here?" I know she couldn't have hitched a ride this time of night, out here in the middle of nowhere. I only passed one vehicle myself, a dark-colored Jag XJ12. Nice, but I wasn't surprised to see a British car broken down on the side of the road. I felt kind of bad about not stopping to help the old guy.

The girl laughs like she's gotten away with something big. "I told my folks I needed the Explorer to go to a friend's house to study." She points to a gently sloping bank by the river. "I drove it right into the water. It might even make it to Virginia before anybody finds it."

"So how come you didn't just go down with the ship?" There's no way I want to be entombed in this pile of junk, but a late-model sports utility vehicle wouldn't be so bad. My glasses are starting to fog up and I take them off.

"Because I don't want them to find me." I can just make out that she's picking at the yarn.

"Why not?" I put my glasses back on.

"None of your business." Suddenly, she grabs the envelope from the dash and turns on the overhead light. I grab her wrist.

"Give that back."

"Ouch, you're hurting me. All right, take it." She rubs her wrist. "What do you care if I look at it? You must want somebody to read it."

"It's a matter of timing. You wouldn't understand." I wish I could speak as well as Poe wrote. *From childhood's hour I have not been as others were; I have not seen as others saw; I could not bring my passions from a common spring.* My old man was a master of timing. I still remember that day in fifth grade when I woke up and he was gone. Pretty smooth maneuver. He wasn't the one that had to deal with a bawling kid.

"So how come I've never seen you at school?" I ask her. She's the kind of girl you can't help but notice. By the light of the car, I see that her eyes are brown. Mine are hardly any color. I put "frostbite blue" on my driver's license application, but the clerk just scratched through it and wrote "light" instead.

"I go to the Christian school."

"Oh." I pretty much gave up on God about the time Mom gave up hope of ever seeing any child support checks, and moved us into a used trailer.

The AMC sputters and quits. Out of gas. Don't need a full tank for a one-way trip. "So where's your religion now?" I say, mostly to fill the space of sound. She turns her head to the passenger window. Then I see her hand, the one with the ring, creep down to rest on her belly. *And, though my faith be broken, and though my heart be broken, here is a ring, as token.*

"You're pregnant." I'll sink into my watery grave a virgin.

"Yeah, that's right, Sherlock." Her hand drops to her lap.

"So what? It's not that big a deal." Happens to plenty of girls at my school.

She turns her head and fires a stare at me that says I'm the biggest idiot in the world. "I'd say the minister's daughter getting pregnant is a pretty big deal."

"Well, what about forgiveness and all that other stuff?"

Her eyes fill with tears. "You just don't get it. I have to be the perfect one. For the perfect family. For the perfect new brick church."

I can't stand to see a female cry. "Can't you just go ahead and marry your boyfriend?"

"He said--" Her voice breaks. "He said he couldn't be sure it was his! He even asked for his ring back. I told him he'd have to pry it from my cold, dead body. I don't know what made me say that." Then she starts sobbing.

I just sit there while she cries. I can't think of anything to say. It's starting to get cold in the car. I feel bad for this girl, but I feel even sorrier for this baby that nobody wants.

"You have to give your kid a chance," I finally say.

"The baby, the baby! Think of the baby!" Her voice is ugly and mocking, but she stops crying. "I drove to an abortion clinic once with my parents. I was hollering right along with all the other protesters. Never gave a thought to what those women were going through. Well, I guess this is my punishment."

"Maybe I'd have been better off if I'd never been born." I watch the words leave my mouth on little wisps of fog. It's so cold. "My dad sure didn't want me."

The girl wipes her eyes with the backs of her hands. "You left that note for him?"

"I don't even know where he is." I touch the envelope again. It's the only thing that seems real tonight. "This is for my mom. I don't want her blaming herself."

"You're not such a bad guy. I mean, that's kind of sweet, you thinking of your mom's feelings." She frowns. "So what's your deal, anyway?"

"I just don't see the point." *All that we see or seem is but a dream within a dream.*

"Well, don't you have plans after school?"

I consider telling her about my poetry, but I've never shown my stuff to anybody. It's no good, just a weird blend of Poe and Jim Morrison. "Hell, I'll never amount to anything," I say.

That's what my dad said, the night before he left. I was in bed, but I could hear them fighting. I couldn't sleep anyway. I just lay there, rubbing my jaw where it throbbed. I'd been gawking at a crow flying over me in the outfield when the ball smacked me so hard I fell down. I heard Mom saying she was taking me out of Little League. Dad told her it was my own fault for not paying attention. "That boy doesn't have a lick of common sense," he said. "You baby him too much." Then Mom started screaming, "He's not cut out to be an athlete. Can't you see that? Or maybe you're too busy trying to make him just like you." Dad got even louder. "No danger of that, the way you interfere every time I try to show him how to be a man. Hell, you keep clucking over him, he'll never amount to anything." That was the last thing I heard my daddy say. Mom slammed into the bathroom and started crying. My door opened and I called, "Dad?" But nobody came in. "Dad?" The door closed, leaving me alone in the dark.

I check my watch. "Midnight."

For awhile, neither of us moves. Finally, she says, "Let's do it together." She opens the door and gets out.

I turn off the overhead light -- no reason Mom should have to fool with a dead battery, too -- and follow her to the crest of the bridge. I had been a little worried that the water might be iced over, but the river is so gorged with melted snow that it makes a whooshing sound as it rushes over the rocks. The black water winks at me in the moonlight.

We stand there, looking down, down at the water. *I stand amid the roar of a surf-tormented shore.* "Wow," she says. "This is it."

"Yeah."

I feel her take my hand. "I'm scared." Her voice squeaks like a little girl. "How about you?"

"Yeah." But I'm starting to feel numb from the cold. And too much thinking. I stare at the river. It's calling to me, pulling me from the bridge. I don't have to jump. All I have to do is lean forward. With my free hand, I push my glasses up on my nose. I want to see where I'm going. *They fell: for Heaven to them no hope imparts who hear not for the beating of their hearts.*

A jerk at my wrist stops me. I turn to see the girl clutching her stomach. "Wow," she says.

"What's wrong?"

She flops down on the concrete, hands still on her belly. "I think I felt the baby." I drop down beside her. My rear end starts to congeal into an ice cube, but we just sit there, listening to the river tumbling below us. The moon throws a weird silver light over the bridge and bare trees. Then I remember a whisper from that dark night, something I'd buried under all those angry words. A sigh, and then, "Good night, little Buddy." That was the last thing my dad said to me.

"I don't think I want to do this," the girl says. I look at her, seeing something soft in her face for the first time. "How about you?"

I try to think of something meaningful to say about the miracle of life, that maybe there's such as thing as faith separate from religion. *A crucifix needs walls, spirit soars* -- nah. Instead I come out with, "Well, my schedule's all blown to hell, anyway." We scramble away from the edge of the bridge. "But I've got to give the river something tonight." She follows me to the car, then back to the bridge, where I tear up the envelope and letter. The confetti floats to the water like snow.

"I've got something for the river, too." She yanks the ring from her hand and hurls it into the current. For a moment, her face shines in the night. Then she looks scared again. "My folks are going to skin me when they find out about the Explorer."

"No, you got a good game plan going," I tell her. "They'll be too freaked about the Ford to bug you about the baby. At least for awhile."

"You're pretty cheerful for a jumper." But she smiles.

I want to say something about how the new life in her represents hope, that maybe things will turn out all right for both of us. But all I say is, "Yeah, well, how are we going to get home?"

She smiles at me again, and takes my hand. "Now we walk back."

I perched at the edge of night
Under a moon blazing cold
Preparing to sluice my life
Into a river black as coal.

I perched at the edge of night
Seeking the water's embrace
Instead, I found hope in another's eyes
And for myself, a measure of grace.

--Johnnie Ray Sowers, 1998

The Ring

Today is my wedding anniversary, but I don't have a wife.

I still have the ring, though. It catches a stray break of sunshine and glows as I drive my route on a rotten March day in this dark brown UPS truck, trying to watch for icy patches. The ring weighs on me, troubles me, yet I can't bring myself to take it off. I'm not sure who I'd be without this gold band. Never considered there might come a time when Rhonda wouldn't be in my life. That she wouldn't want me. That she wouldn't love me the way she must have when she made $20 installment payments on this ring.

Even after I found out she was cheating on me, I tried to work things out. It wasn't in my nature to quit. I was happy being part of a matched set. It wasn't in Rhonda's nature to stick around. She said it drove her crazy knowing that for the rest of her life, every Tuesday we would sit at the kitchen table and pay the bills and every Friday we'd order a pizza and rent a video. I said we could go out to eat and see a movie, but she took off out West with some long-haired guy making half a living airbrushing custom scenes on vans. She sued me for mental cruelty, although as far as I know, my biggest crime was being too steady. I wish I could have opened myself up and shown the judge my insides, how my soul had come to resemble something chewed by a WeedEater.

The papers were signed and filed months ago. But to take this ring off would make it official that I failed as a husband. That I wasn't man enough to satisfy my wife. I'm still not ready to face an empty hand.

I pull into a driveway and run to the door with a package. I ring the bell and hightail it back to the truck. I try not to get caught at houses -- people always want to talk, and it puts me behind schedule. The old ladies never can understand the concept of an electronic signature. I hand them the clipboard and stylus, and every time they say, "What am I supposed to do with this?"

My sister tells me to shuck this ring, to announce my availability. I'm still a young man at thirty-five, I can find someone else, even raise a family. That's what she tells me, but I don't aim to let myself in for that kind of hurt again. Besides, what does she know? She's not married, except to her chiropractic practice. Because she was born a few minutes before me, she thinks she knows what's best for both of us.

There was that old girlfriend from high school, but that was just a warm body, a chance connection. I'd run into her at McDonald's. She was buying a Happy Meal for her son, a strange, quiet child. "Hey," she said, running her fingers through her bright blonde hair. "I hear you're a free man." I saw her a couple of times, but it bothered me to walk to the bedroom with her, leaving her little boy sitting silently at the kitchen table with his coloring book and crayons. Being with her made me feel even more lonely.

I swear that damn ring is winking at me, reminding me that I'll never be free. I pull up to my sister's office for a pickup and walk inside to find some old guy leaning against the counter in the lobby. "Look, Louise, I need to get going."

"Hold on, Thomas, I got to give you a printout." Louise, who's near retirement age, is trying to learn the new computer with all these codes for various chiropractic services. "Well, hell." She hauls off and slams the monitor with her fist. Then she looks up at me. "You didn't see that."

"See what?" I have to smile. "My sister around?"

"Yeah, I think she's in her office. Go on back."

I walk down the hall and open the office door to find Madeline putting a golf ball into a urine specimen cup. She stops and grins at me, pushing back that wild red hair that mirrors her temperament. My dark looks suit my personality. The only features we share are blue eyes and what our mom calls a stubbornness of jaw and disposition.

"I wouldn't mind having a job like this," I tell her.

"I'll lend you the catalog that I ordered my diploma from," she says.

"So, you just see your patients whenever you feel like it, huh?"

"For your information, one patient is receiving ultrasound, I've ordered moist heat for another and the new patient is still getting x-rayed. So I'm taking a few minutes to relax, and when I step out of this office, I'll be refreshed and even more attentive to my patients." She cocks her head at me. "You ever heard of relaxation? You ought to try it, just once."

"It's against my religion. I was going to see if you wanted to grab some lunch, but it looks like you'll be here awhile. Especially at the rate you're going."

"Don't let the door hit you on your way out," she says, giving me her evil-sister smile. "Hey, wait a minute." She grabs my arm. "Why is this still on your hand? I thought we talked about this."

"You talked about it."

Madeline holds out her hand. "Give it here."

"What?"

"Take it off." She snaps her fingers.

"Look, Maddening--"

"I'm serious. Take it off for five seconds. If you don't like the feel of fresh air, you can put it right back on." She locks those I-am-your-twin-do-my-bidding eyes on me.

"You're a nut."

"Who's wearing the white coat and who's wearing institutional brown?"

I don't know why, but I start tugging on the ring. That's all I can do, though. "It won't come off."

"Nice try."

"No, I can't get it past my knuckle." I thought I was in pretty good shape. Wonder when that weight snuck up on me.

"Come with me." Madeline leads me to an examining room sink and hands me a bottle of foul-smelling liquid soap. "Here, wash your hands in cold water with this. It should slide right off." It doesn't. Madeline squats and roots around in the cabinet until she finds a bottle of mineral oil. "Hold your hand over the sink." She lubricates my finger and tries to work the band along my skin. It won't budge past the knuckle. Suddenly, I desperately want to rid myself of this ring. Now it seems like a cancerous growth.

With bad intent, she asks, "Do you really use that finger much?"

"I'm right attached to it, Dr. Maddening."

"Pity." She folds her arms across her chest and stares at me until an aha-look appears in those blue eyes. From the counter, she grabs a small brown bottle of liquid with a silver trigger on the top.

"What's that?" It looks like something I don't want to mess with.

"Fluori-Methane. Give me your hand."

"What's it for?"

"It's used to manage restricted motion, muscle spasms and such." That doesn't sound bad. I offer my hand. "Hold still." She upends the bottle, squeezes the trigger and shoots a stream of liquid on my finger.

"That's cold as ice!"

"Yes, if you apply too much, you can cause frostbite."

I jerk my hand back and start working the ring. It moves farther up my finger than before, but it can't quite clear that fat knuckle.

"Leverage. That's what we need," my sister says. She points to the floor. "Sit there with your back to the wall."

"I'm not doing any such thing." She's as crazy as her red hair.

"Fine." I can't believe she would retreat that easily. "By the way, can you feel where that ring is cutting off your circulation?" Visions of gangrene skip through my mind and I drop to the floor, back to the wall.

Madeline sits in front of me, Indian-style, and motions for me to do the same. Then she plants her feet against the wall, grabs my finger and starts pulling.

"Hey, that hurts!"

She grunts and keeps tugging. "Hold on--" She yanks at me even harder, and the next thing I know, I'm tumbling through the air, doing an acrobatic flip over her and landing on my backside on the carpet. I had no idea she was that strong.

"Damn it to hell, Mad--" I stop when I see her sitting there, hair in her face, laughing and waving the gold band.

"You're a free man," she says.

I do feel relieved. But there's still a ring on my finger, a pinched circle of unnaturally white flesh. Everything I've lost remains right in front of me. My throat tightens and I choke down the sob that's trying to bust out of me.

Madeline stops smiling and drops the ring in her coat pocket. "What's wrong?" She scoots over to where I'm sitting on the floor. I just shake my head and pinch my eyes shut. I will not lose control. "You're better off without her, Billy."

"Why couldn't she love me?" I paw for a handkerchief in my pocket and blow my nose, hard. I'm not crying. "That's all I want to know. Why wasn't I worth being faithful to?"

Madeline grabs my hands and holds them to her heart, the way she did when were kids and she wanted to tell me something important. One time it was to say she was doomed to hell because she'd killed a bird with a rock. Another time it was to confide that she planned to be one of the first moon colonists. Years later, it was to tell me she was going away to Iowa to school. "Billy, what she did isn't about you. She'll always be looking for something she could have had all along."

I open my eyes and look at my sister. "Mad, I feel like a piece of me has been cut out. Like I'll never be whole again."

Her face becomes very still. "That's exactly how I felt on your wedding day. I felt like we had been cut apart." She looks at me steadily. "But that twin thing, it's eternal. You look deep into that hole in your heart. I'm still there."

I feel the warmth of her hand covering that bare finger. I look into the face of my sister, and see love and acceptance of the man I am right now. I stare into those blue eyes and I begin to see myself again.

The intercom squawks and I hear a mumbled, "Hellfire--" Then, louder, "Doc, where are you? The screen just went blank, I don't know, I might have hit, 'delete' or something--"

Madeline winks at me and gets up. She presses the intercom button and tells Louise, "Don't touch another key, I'll be right there." By the time she turns around, I'm up, too, brushing lint off my dark pants.

"The wildfires are calling," she says.

"You better get going. Your victims -- I mean, your patients -- are waiting."

She pauses at the door. "You going to be all right?"

"Yeah," I say. "Yeah, I am."

Madeline stops in the doorway, pats her coat pocket and retrieves the ring. "What do you want done with this?"

I hadn't thought that far ahead.

"Wonder what one of these would look like on me?" Madeline, who wears only a watch as jewelry, slips the ring on her finger. "Nah, it's just not me." She starts to remove the band. "I don't believe this." She yanks on the ring. "It's stuck."

I start laughing. "Well, I gotta get back to work. See you." I squeeze past her and head down the hall.

"You get back here and help me!"

"Don't worry," I call back as I keep walking. "It takes awhile before it starts to cut off your circulation."

Valentine

I don't know why I have to give valentines to the boys in my class. My brother is a boy, and I can't stand him.

"Keesha, you can't give cards just to some of the kids," Mommy says. "The others will feel left out." So I tear open the package Mommy bought at the store and make two piles: pretty cards for the girls and ugly cards for the boys.

Next, I write all the names on the envelopes. Now that I'm in second grade, I can print pretty good. Sometimes I get words mixed up, but Mommy says I'll grow out of it. I'm not so sure. I'm afraid to tell her that sometimes the letters look backwards, too. I think there might be something wrong with my brain.

OK. Now to pick out the cards. Ooh, here's the prettiest one. The picture is a skunk, but it's as pretty as a kitty cat, all black and white with a big, big fluffy tail. It's sitting in a garden full of yellow, pink and blue flowers. The skunk hugs a huge heart that says, "Hi, Valentine!" I'm giving this one to my best friend, Shawna.

OK. This is the ugliest one. It's a pitiful little duck with part of an eggshell on its head. "Just Bursting to Wish You a Happy Valentine's Day!" That is so stupid. It's perfect for Sammy.

Mommy thinks he's cute just because he hugged her when she brought cupcakes to our class for Halloween. She took a day off work just for me. "He's got the biggest brown eyes," she said.

Sammy drives me crazy. And it's not just me. He bugs all the kids because he argues about everything. We got into a big fight on the school bus one time. He turned around in the seat in front of me. "Keesha, what's your middle name?"

"April, not that it's any of your business."

"I know how to spell that, it's just like the month. A-P-R-I-L." He grinned at me, sticking his fingers in his mouth and jiggling the loose tooth in front. Gross.

"No, it's A-P-R-Y-L."

"Wrong. It's A-P-R-I-L." He's just like my brother, thinks he's so smart.

"I guess I know how to spell my own name," I said. "It's A-P-R-Y-L."

"Can't be. All the calendars say A-P-R-I-L."

"It's A-P-R-Y-L," I said, getting madder. And louder. "A-P-R-Y-L!" The driver stopped the bus and made me move to the front seat. "Wait, he--" I tried to explain, but the driver wouldn't listen to me.

We get to have a snack while the teacher hands out the valentines. Sammy's mom made cookies shaped like hearts and decorated them with pink and red icing. She's real nice. "Don't your braids look pretty, Keesha?" his mom whispers, her breath warm in my ear as she sets a napkin full of cookies on my desk.

I wiggle my nose, pretending I'm a rabbit. The cookies smell sweet. I nibble one in little bunny bites. Sammy, who sits beside me, stuffs food as fast as he can. Ugh, he's got a milk mustache. Gross. I check out Shawna, who sits right in front of me. Good, she's opening my card. Oh, no! She's holding the duck card. That means--

"Wow!" That's Sammy hollering and waving the skunk for everybody to see. "Thanks, Keesha!" Everybody, and I mean everybody, in the room is laughing at me. Sammy's mom has her hand over her mouth, but I know she's laughing, too.

"Shawna, I didn't mean, you were supposed to get --" But the teacher tells us to quieten down and clear our desks for recess.

"Hey, Keesha!" Sammy waves at me across the playground. I act like I don't hear him and climb on the monkey bars. Ooh, I should have put my gloves on. The metal is so cold. But I like the sound of my hands slapping the bars.

Sammy's waiting for me when I drop to the ground. "Your shoe's untied," he says.

I don't say anything, hoping he'll go away so I can find the teacher. I still can't tie my shoes by myself. It's like the letters. I can make the loops, but when I try to bring them together, everything seems backwards.

"You going to tie your shoe?" He stands there with his mouth open, wiggling that stupid tooth.

"I'll tie it when I feel like it."

"You'd better tie it now," Sammy says. "You could trip and hurt yourself."

"You're not my boss."

He won't give up. "Why don't you just go ahead and tie it?"

"Because I can't!" My nose starts to run and my eyes feel wet, but I won't cry.

"You can't tie your shoes?" Sammy looks at me like I just told him I couldn't brush my teeth.

"My brother says I'm stupid." I don't have a tissue, so I wipe my nose on the arm of my jacket.

"You're not stupid," Sammy says. "You just need practice. Here, let me show you." He gets down on his knees and ties my shoe.

"That's what my grandpa says, I just need practice." Then, something about Sammy at my feet makes me giggle.

"What's so funny?" Sammy is still on his knees, looking up at me.

"I don't know, it's like I'm a queen and you're my servant."

Sammy grins. "Queens and kings have people do everything for them. Even getting dressed." He stands and bows. "I will be your shoe servant, my queen."

Sammy's mom shows up with ear muffs. "How many times have I told you to keep those ears covered?" Sammy squawks and wriggles, but she jams those ears muffs on him. Then she smiles at me. "My boy picked the prettiest girl in class for his girlfriend."

I smile back at her, but I don't say anything. "I believe you're a little shy," she says. Sometimes parents can be pretty dumb. I'm not his girlfriend. I'm his queen.

The Well Ain't Dry Yet

I've come home to West Virginia to die. These mountains have called me to my final resting place. I'm going to enjoy the dogwoods this spring, eat vine-ripened tomatoes this summer and watch the leaves turn gold and red. Then I'll ease away before winter settles. I'm getting too old to lift a shovel or fool with that kerosene heater every time a heavy snow sends tree limbs crashing against power lines.

My arteries must have started hardening for me to ever leave the mountains where I grew up. But when my daughter called and found out I'd been without electricity for five days, she didn't have to argue very long before I agreed to move to Florida to live with her.

At first, it was a relief to leave that cold and empty house. I thought I'd leave my sorrowful memories, too. I kept expecting to find Bessie at the electric range, stirring a pot of beans. Or shooing me outside, so she could mop. I'd turn off the eleven o'clock news and walk into the bedroom, where she'd be sitting up in bed, reading her Bible. And every time, her absence would hit me fresh. She wasn't there. I was never going to see her again. I had such a foolish desire to reach out and touch her.

Sweet Bessie. I was a better man with her. Oh, we had our problems over the years. She was always after me to hold my tongue. I always thought she was a little too mindful of other people's opinions. And she wouldn't let me touch her at night until she finished reading her Bible chapter. Once I remarked that it looked to me like one pass through the book ought to be enough, and I spent a lonely night on my side of the bed. Waking up without her hand on my chest was even more lonesome. I still miss the warmth of that gentle pressure. I didn't figure I'd last the year without her. Well, it won't be much longer. It's just about time.

I sure as hell didn't want to die in Florida. Too many Yankees. I didn't mind them when I worked as a doorman at the Birch Falls resort. Yankees are very generous when they've just had a good round of golf and better drinks. "Thomas, you're a good man," they'd say, palming a big bill into my hand. "Yes, sir," I always said, standing straight in my dark green uniform and matching cap. They never knew that little knot of anger I carried with me, smiling at the door to a facility where I was not allowed to be a guest. When I was a young man, I wanted to be a carpenter, to work with my hands. To build something that would last. Something fine. It was just a foolish notion. Didn't have any way of learning the trade. I had to settle on a steady wage to support my family.

When my daughter came to take me to Florida, she treated me to lunch at Birch Falls, just to prove that times have changed. We both had the special, some kind of broiled fish. I sat there in that flowered-up room, drinking ice water out of a dark blue goblet. I might be allowed, but I still didn't belong there.

Found out I didn't belong in Florida, either. "Don't leave, Daddy," my daughter begged, but we never spent much time together. She worked long hours, and her idea of an outing was to park me on a courtyard bench while she poked around shops full of things nobody needs. If I'd had Bessie by my side, maybe I could have been more content. I didn't tell my daughter I was dying. I just said I was tired of

Florida and all the old people chasing youth like guinea hens pecking for corn.

Her youngest, Yolanda, came for me. Said she'd missed me and would love for me to come live with her. She rents a house that's not much to look at. It's just a little white frame with a sad-looking porch, but I wonder that she can afford it. I think her mother sends her money, and I'm giving her part of my Social Security check.

Yolanda is a good girl. Works hard as an LPN. She'll get a phone call from the hospital, asking her to fill in for somebody's shift, and off she goes. She hands out medicine, takes the bedpan around, even gives enemas. I couldn't handle being that intimate with strangers -- I kept my distance when I was a doorman. Yolanda says she doesn't mind, because she's helping people. Sometimes she helps patients get better. Sometimes, she helps them die. She makes sure to turn them in their beds, so they don't have to suffer from sores. It's good those people have somebody like Yolanda to comfort them. But that's not how I'm going out. When it's time, I'm either going to keel over on my feet, or I'm just going to sleep and not wake up. I ain't about to linger all feeble and drooling.

Yolanda has her grandmother's wide, dark eyes and round figure. But she's not content with herself. When she came to pick me up in Florida, her hair was as straight as Bessie's garden rows. "What have you done to yourself, girl?" I asked.

"I just used a relaxer, Grandpa," she giggled.

"What was wrong with the way it was growing out of your head?"

"Nothing. I just wanted a change."

Shame she ain't married. She needs a flock of children, the way she fusses and worries over me. "Grandpa, are you comfortable?" she kept asking on the trip back to West Virginia. "You need the bathroom?" To tell you the truth, I usually did. My prostate was acting up.

Now she's taken a notion that I need to go to a chiropractor. I was enjoying a piece of her chocolate pie after supper when she lit into me. "You move so stiff, Grandpa."

"Well, I ain't no spring chicken." Perfect, sky-high meringue, just like Bessie used to make. Yolanda stood up and removed the pie from the table. "I thought I might have another piece."

"You probably need to start watching your sugar." I am discovering pretty quick that old people and children are treated like second-class citizens. Everybody feels free to make decisions for us.

Yolanda didn't even ask me before she made the appointment. "I won't go," I told her.

"Come on, Grandpa, she might be able to help you." Yolanda held out a fresh-pressed shirt.

"She?" I thought I'd choke on my dentures. "You want me to see some quack that ain't even a real doctor, and a female at that? No woman's cracking my neck."

"Grandpa." She laid her hand on my arm, just like Bessie used to do. "I want you to be here a long time. Do it for me. Please."

So here I am, sitting in a waiting room with the rest of the sheep ready for slaughter. My name is called and I get up. Yolanda rises, too. She's got another new hairstyle. Chopped off all that shiny long hair. "You stay right there," I tell her.

"Are you sure you don't need me to help?" She looks at me anxiously.

"I think I can handle it by myself," I say.

The chiropractor is a pretty little redhead. "Hello, Thomas," she says. It really irritates me how doctors feel free to call their elders by their first names.

I squint at the patch on her coat. "Hello, Madeline." I can see she doesn't like that. Good. "Look, I'm going to save us both some time. My granddaughter means well, but there's no point in my being here."

"Really?" She raises her eyebrows.

"This is just between you and me. I'm dying. I've accepted it. I don't need to be poked and prodded my last days."

I expect her to say something like, "You poor man." Instead, the doctor just stares at me with her bright blue eyes. "What makes you think you're dying?"

"I feel it in my blood and in my bones," I tell her. "Everything is slowing down. It's just a matter of time."

"Maybe you're right," she says, surprising me again. "But you're here and I'm here, and your daughter is expecting some kind of answer, so how about you let me do an exam, anyway?"

"Don't you go trying to crack my neck." If Bessie were with me, she'd lay her hand softly on my arm and say, "Now, Thomas." She could always calm me. And if I didn't settle down, she'd dig those fingers in my flesh until I shut up.

The doctor laughs and starts looking me over. She folds my arms and legs in funny positions, then asks me to push, like she wants to see what my muscles will do. She uses some kind of measuring instrument on my spine. Next thing I know, an even younger woman is parading me down the hall to the x-ray room, my paper gown flapping for anybody that wants a look at my withered glory. Then I'm back in the examining room, and the doctor smiles at me.

"Thomas," she says. "You're not dying. You do show evidence of osteoarthritis, but mostly, you're just out of shape."

"Young lady, I am eighty years old."

"Do you do any kind of exercise?"

"I've been retired almost twenty years." I deserve the rest, too.

"I take that as a 'no.' " She scribbles on a chart. "How's your diet?"

"Well, I still have a good appetite." I'm pretty proud of that. Nobody has to force feed me some chalky vitamin drink.

"Do you eat a lot of sweets?"

"I enjoy a good homemade pie or cake." She scribbles some more and heads for the door. "I'll be right back." Uh oh. I don't think I like where this is going.

The doctor returns with Yolanda. Hell. "Your grandfather would benefit from daily walks," she says. "It's weight-bearing exercise that helps build bone mass." Yolanda nods. "But I need your help, too. He needs to eat more fresh foods, and he really needs to cut down on the sweets." Yolanda nods again. "I'd like to give him an adjustment--"

"You can talk directly to me," I interrupt. "And I can tell you right now I ain't letting you pop my bones."

"Now, Grandpa," Yolanda begins to whine.

"A lot of patients have anxiety about adjustments at first," the doctor says. "Let me give you some literature to take home." She steps behind me to a rack and hands Yolanda a couple of brochures. Then she rests her hands on my shoulders and pats me like she's soothing a baby. "I have a feeling you'll be here to welcome your great-grandchildren," she says. Next thing I know, my head is hanging to one side. Then she snaps it around the other way.

"There," she says. "That's better."

"I could sue you." But I feel like I'm sitting up more straight.

The doctor grins at me. "Go ahead. I dare you to live long enough for the case to come to trial."

The ordeal starts that evening, at supper. I was planning on finishing off that pie, but instead, Yolanda sets in front of me a bowl of chopped apples, bananas, grapes and pineapple. "What's this?"

"Dessert. Fruit salad." I might be dying, but I wasn't planning on this much suffering.

"My dentures can't handle this apple peel."

"Well, you can eat the other fruit."

After she washes up the dishes, she comes and stands in front of the game show I'm trying to watch on television. "Let's take a walk."

"I'm too tired."

"Please, Grandpa. Just a little stroll." I might as well go ahead and give in. I won't get any peace either way.

Yolanda lives on a street with more children and cats than cars, so it's a decent walk. I have to admit the warm breeze feels good on my face. It's been a cold spring, but now leaves are starting to appear on the trees and tulips wave from yards.

"This is nice," Yolanda says, stopping to smell a purple blossom on a neighbor's lilac bush. "It reminds me of Grandma." I sniff the air and I can see Bessie in the morning, reaching for that bottle of toilet water. "I still miss her."

"I do, too, honey." I want to paw at the air, just to see if I could feel her spirit.

"Grandpa, I don't mean to fuss at you. I really don't. You just mean so much to me."

I never have known how to answer when women start talking about their feelings. Finally, I say, "I don't know how you put up with an old grouch like me."

"You're my grandpa," she says.

I start walking again. Yolanda keeps talking. "You and Grandma did so much for me. I remember how hard it was for me when I started school. I was the slowest one in the whole class, and Momma worked so much that she didn't have much time to help me." I remember her as a little girl, her face all pinched and anxious. Bessie could always make her smile, with a hug or a cookie or a story. "Time. I couldn't even get that straight, what the big hand and little hand was all about. It was Grandma that taught me with that clock in the kitchen." Yolanda stops and points. "Your shoe is untied."

"So it is." I stare down at it. I know I can't bend to tie it. If I try, I probably won't be able to get back up.

Yolanda looks at me and then I see understanding in her eyes. Quickly, she squats and ties the lace. When she's done, I start walking again, head turned from her. Yolanda follows. "It was you that taught me how to do that. I thought I must be the stupidest girl in the world because I couldn't figure out how to tuck those loops and tie a knot. But you just kept showing me over and over. You never yelled, you just smiled and said practice makes perfect." I don't remember ever being that patient. Must have been my doorman personality. I believe I must have shed that with my uniform when I retired.

The doctor acts like she's looking for something. "I don't see the gun to your head," she says. "Yet here you are."

I am determined that my granddaughter is not going to tie my shoelaces for me in public. But I'm not telling this woman any of that. "I'm just here to make Yolanda happy."

"Do you have any particular complaints today? I mean, besides the specter of death, of course."

She's trying to get a smile out of me, but I won't give her the satisfaction. "I thought I'd see if you had some kind of adjustment to loosen up my back a little." She helps me lie on my stomach on some kind of padded table. I brace myself for a big crack, but her hands gently push here and there on my back, and then she starts moving the bottom half of the table up and down. I believe she calls it traction. I feel my spine opening up like a newly-lubricated hinge.

Usually, after supper, I like to spend the rest of the evening watching shows, but I feel like going outside today. Yolanda is making herself a turkey sandwich to take to work tomorrow. "You ready to walk?"

"Oh, maybe I'll let you off the hook this time, Grandpa." She puts the sandwich in the refrigerator and sits down at the kitchen table. "I'm pretty wiped this evening. I feel all bloated. It's just about that time of the--"

I cut her off before she can share any more of her female condition. "Just a little stroll," I suggest. "I'll slow my pace so you can keep up with me."

Before I know it, I've got a whole new routine. I'm eating more roughage than a farm animal, and I'm walking every day and seeing the chiropractor every couple of weeks. She says eating less sugar gives me more energy to exercise and that the walking is making me stronger.

"I'm still eighty years old," I tell her. "You can't turn back the clock. I won't see another spring."

"You're a widower, aren't you?" Those shiny blue eyes lock on me. "It would be natural if you experienced some depression--"

I know she's going to suggest I see a counselor. "Just hold it right there. I'm not going to lay on a couch and tell my personal business to some stranger. And I don't see what this has to do with my spine, anyway."

"You're not just a collection of symptoms, Thomas," she says. "I try to see the whole person." She scribbles on a piece of paper and hands it to me. "St. John's Wort. It's an herb that seems to work without side effects. You can pick it up at the health food store."

I have no intention of taking that stuff, but the office calls Yolanda at work, just in case I "let it slip my mind." Try it for a month, she wheedles. She hands the pill to me with my breakfast juice, like I can't be trusted to take it on my own. She's right.

I can't tell that the pills make any difference. I'm too busy to really pay attention. Now, after Yolanda goes to work, I take a morning walk, too. Anymore, I'm the one that has to nag her to get going. She's gone and ruined her hair again. She calls the color champagne blonde. I can't understand why she wants to look like a white woman.

"Grandpa, I've got something to tell you," she says one evening as we're walking. "But you're going to be disappointed in me."

"Go ahead and tell me." I bet she's lost her job. So many places are cutting back these days.

"I can't. I'm too ashamed." Her face is wet.

"Might as well tell me."

"I'm pregnant." She digs a tissue out of her pocket and blows her nose.

"Well." I don't know what I ought to say. I didn't even know she had a boyfriend. I guess she was meeting him when I thought she was working overtime. "Is he going to marry you?"

She shakes her head. "He always said he was just waiting for the divorce to come through, but when I told him about the baby, I found out he hadn't even filed the papers." So this is why she never brought him around. She wipes at her eyes with the back of her hands. "I am so stupid."

I can't stand it when she does that, putting herself down and ready to give up. I can see that little girl, struggling to tie those shoelaces. "I can't do it, Grandpa," she would cry. "I'm too stupid."

"What do you *want* to do?"

She looks at me, those wide brown eyes opening even more, like she's never considered that she has a choice. "I want this baby. I don't know if I'll be a good mother, but I want this baby."

I wish Bessie were here to comfort this girl. I manage to pat Yolanda's back. "You'll be a good mother. Just promise me one thing."

"What's that?"

"I don't want to hear you calling yourself 'stupid' ever again."

"But that's how I feel--" Those eyes are begging me to let her keep the comfort of doubting herself.

"You come from fine women. You got that strength and wisdom in you. You just got to look inside yourself and find it." She nods her head and I see her hand creep to her belly, as though to check on the promise there. "A baby. That's a fine thing."

Then it occurs to me that a baby and an old man are too many burdens for one young woman. "You'll be needing my room."

"No, Grandpa, you can't leave me! I need you."

"I'm still planning on giving you that money from my check. You'll need it for the baby."

Yolanda grabs my arm. "That's not what I mean. I need *you*, Grandpa."

I came home to West Virginia to die, but now I don't have time. Little Bessie keeps me busy. The old hens at church informed me that I had no business trying to babysit at my age. "Don't bury me before my time," I told them. "The well ain't dry yet."

It's not so hard. Thanks to the chiropractor, I can bend over the changing table. I can straighten back up, too. These days, you don't even have to fool with pins to get a diaper on a baby. She's not a fussy child, anyway. Every bit as sweet-natured as her great-grandmother. I rest when she rests. I've been whittling a little, trying to fashion a kitten out of maple. Thought Little Bessie might enjoy playing with it when she gets a little older. Might try my hand at making her a set of baby animals.

The old hens warned me not to spoil her, but I sit and rock her hour after hour while Yolanda is at work. I wrap my great-granddaughter in a small quilt made by a woman nearly one hundred years old, from pieces of Bessie's bright aprons. The little girl smiles and coos at me like she knows exactly who I am. She's a beautiful child, with those wide, brown eyes shining from a face that's just the way I like my coffee -- black and strong, with a little cream. Sometimes I fancy that Bessie's spirit has returned in this tiny vessel. For so long, I yearned for my wife's comfort, to touch her once more. When that little finger grabs mine, I believe I do.

Road Trip

I love taking road trips.

You wouldn't think an insurance claims adjuster would even venture out on the highway, knowing it's loaded with drunks and other assorted idiots. But I've loved the road ever since I was a little girl, riding with my Barbie dolls in the back seat of my parents' Electra on the way to Myrtle Beach. "Look, Angelica," Dad would call back to me. "See those horses over there in that field?" The car smelled strongly of Aqua Velvet aftershave lotion.

Sometimes I could talk Dad into stopping at a souvenir stand and buying me junk. I still remember that water-filled plastic globe with a little beach scene inside. I felt like a magician when I shook the globe and watched the little particles swirl around the striped umbrellas and palmettos. I wonder what happened to it.

I also remember that hateful alligator box from when I was very little. "How can they put an alligator in here?" I asked Dad as I slid back the lid. A tiny wooden alligator head on a spring lunged at me. I screamed and dropped the box. Then I started bawling. I didn't stop until my belly was full of peach ice cream. Mom wiped the ice cream and tears from my face with the wet wash cloth she carried in an old bread wrapper.

Now it's just me and Mom on the road. She's a great companion. She doesn't mind hitting all the rest stops and lingering at the various attractions listed in my AAA guidebooks. A person can learn so much on the road. I'm planning a stop at the capitol in Frankfort, Kentucky, just so I can examine that famous flower clock.

The one condition my mom imposes is that she wants to park and secure her lodging by dark. I can deal with that. Well, she also tends to worry that we're lost. "I don't remember this tunnel," she'll say. "I don't ever remember going past that river."

She used to do that with Dad, too. "Now, Frank, I don't remember seeing that fruit stand before. Are you sure this is the right road?"

"Oh, yeah, I remember it," Dad would say. "Don't you, Angelica?"

"Sure, Daddy," I'd answer, with no remembrance of the fruit stand whatsoever.

"Don't you girls worry about a thing. Just sit back, relax and enjoy the ride."

I wish Dad were here now. I've become more like my mom in the worry department. I worry about people trying to take advantage of her now that she's alone. Actually, I'm a lot like my mom in many ways. Our frames are as stringy as half-runner beans. We both like to get perms before we travel, so we don't have to take time fussing with our hair. But that's where we part company. I get my blonde hair lightly permed so that I won't turn into Medusa. My mother doesn't know about Medusa, and wouldn't care anyway, as long as she gets the most perm for her money. I refuse to attempt to give her a perm, so she asks the beautician for the tightest curl possible. I laugh and call her, "Lambchop," when I pat her wooly white head. We look like a pair of blue-eyed dust mops.

We left Bluefield later than I would have liked, but Mom had to wait for her Social Security check. We're forging up the West Virginia Turnpike in my forest green

Buick. I'm pretty proud of it because it looks a little like one of those big Jags, especially from the rear. Well, mostly from the rear. And in poor light. At least it's not one of those god-awful eggs that pass for car bodies these days. This car's lines flow so elegantly, just as these mountain ridges blend into one another. It's a sunny spring day. The redbuds are blooming in soft lavender. Even the lowly locust trees sprout frothy white sprays. The inside of my car smells like the mountains, too, but that's mainly due to the pine-scented cardboard tree hanging from the rear view mirror.

While I take in the view, Mom's concentrating on the road. Her ten-and-two lock on the steering wheel becomes a death grip as a tractor trailer whooshes by. I'll take over at the next rest stop to negotiate the heavier traffic around Charleston. Besides, Mom will want her hands free to try to capture the golden dome of the capitol with her little automatic camera.

She pulls into the rest stop and closes her eyes for a minute. I suspect she's thanking God for getting her this far. We haul out the grocery bags and cooler and head for a picnic table. Both of us wear windbreakers, because there's a little whisper of a cool breeze. Mom packed hard-boiled eggs, ham biscuits and chocolate oatmeal cookies. I bought miniature carrots, cherry tomatoes, apples, pears and bottled spring water. Mom would have preferred to haul a gallon jar of cold tap water or tea, carried in an old Dixie Crystals sugar bag for insulation.

We bow our heads for a minute, then commence to munching. Mom doesn't hassle me about attending church, and I thank her by showing respect for her beliefs. I don't go to church since Dad died, and I'm not even sure what kind of God I could trust. Now, Mom's faith never wavers. As far as she's concerned, prayer is why she finally bore me in her fourth decade. My folks were so convinced that I was a special gift that I started to feel that they were presents to me. So what kind of God would yank one of them away from me? And give him cancer? And make him suffer so?

Well, there's no point in dwelling on that now. I can't believe we're the only travelers carrying a picnic lunch, but everyone else heads for the fast food concession inside the traveler's pavilion. Some eyeball us with curiosity. I eyeball them right back. I can't stand rude people. "I bet those people wish they were having what we're having."

Mom waggles the biscuit in her hand. "Wonder what I could get for this?"

"Two bucks, easy."

"Looks like a mighty good spread, ladies." Mom drops her biscuit. Fortunately, it falls on a napkin -- it would be a shame to waste one of her tender ham biscuits. I look up to see an older man smiling at us. He's pretty good looking, for an old coot. His thick hair is a pure white, like my mom's, and flows to his collar. His face is lined and tanned from years near the sun. He's wearing a plain black jacket with a white shirt and a bolo tie. His black pants are tucked into exquisitely tooled Western boots polished to perfection.

I turn back to Mom, knowing she is staring straight ahead, like he doesn't exist. She is very cautious about strangers. Me, too. I mean, I like the road, but I've learned plenty about scams. People will say anything to grab a nickel. They'll claim injuries by uninsured -- and invisible -- motorists. They go around wrapped up in bandages and braces, barely able to walk or even sit in a chair. As bad off as they are, they tell us, they're willing to settle reasonably. Then our investigators catch them playing softball or mowing their yards. I know people hate insurance companies, but I swear sometimes I wonder if there is such as thing as an accident.

My mom amazes me by returning the man's smile and saying, "Would you care for some? We have plenty."

"That's awfully kind of you. Don't mind if I do." He settles himself before us. Nervy.

"Here you go." Mom presents him with a paper plate covered with my carrots and tomatoes, two of her biscuits and an egg. She reaches into my cooler and hands him a bottle of water. This beats anything I have ever seen.

"This is just wonderful." The old codger digs into the food with relish. Mom sits there, beaming at him.

"I wish I could offer you some iced tea," Mom says. "I used to always carry some good sweet tea. But I don't bother anymore because the caffeine aggravates Angelica's bladder."

Now it is time for the earth to open up and envelop me, but nary a crack appears. The old fellow swallows and looks at me. "You must be Angelica. Lovely as your mother."

Uh oh. This guy knows his lines. But Mom just smiles and asks, "We're going to visit my cousin in Indiana. Are you going far?" She's too polite to just ask him where's he headed.

"God's country," he answers.

"Oh, that is a long way off." I know that Mom is thinking of Arizona, where one of her brothers lives. The way he's always referring to it as God's country, you'd think it was the state motto. Maybe Mom thinks it is.

He wipes his mouth with his napkin and sips some water. At least he has good table manners. "Today I'm only going as far as Lexington. I want to see a little bit of Kentucky."

"That's where we're stopping for the night!" I can't believe she's sharing such details with a stranger. I nearly choke on my ham biscuit. "Angelica made reservations. She's very good at planning ahead. Do you have reservations?"

"No, ma'am. I'll just stop when the spirit moves me."

"You must have an adventurous spirit." Mom adds more carrot sticks to his plate.

"Yes, I do." He's eyeing the chocolate oatmeal cookies. If he thinks he's going to get his paws on those, he's got another think coming. "And I think you two ladies have kind, generous spirits." Uh huh. Here it comes. Instead, he says, "I can see that you take good care of each other."

I stand up and say, "Mom, we need to get going if we're going to miss rush hour traffic in Charleston."

The old man stands. "Thank you. I wish you ladies a safe and joyous journey." He bows slightly to my mother and walks away. I watch him walk to his vehicle. I feel a little relief to see him walk on by the beat-up, curtained van. He slides into a dark green Jag XJ12 and drives away in the car I wish I could afford. And a V-12 at that. The polish shines. He takes good care of it. All right. He drives a good car. Probably leaks oil, though. Well, maybe he's not an ax murderer. Could be an embezzler.

It feels good to relax in my pajamas in the motel room and read my latest issue of *National Geographic*. You can learn a lot from that magazine. For instance, the male goshawk will deliver prey, plucked and ready for eating, to the incubating female. Mom's washed her face and applied the Oil of Olay. Her teeth sit in a little plastic Tupperware box on the bathroom counter. She's wearing a flannel nightgown as she sits up in bed, peering through her bifocals at a crossword puzzle.

I'm having trouble concentrating on the article. "I still don't understand why you were so friendly to that stranger."

She doesn't even look up from her puzzle. "I already told you that he seemed like a nice man."

"Mom, you have to be careful. Not everybody is as nice as you. People will try to take advantage of you."

"What's a six-letter word for God?" she asks. "I should know that."

"Yahweh. Y-a-h-w-e-h." I'm a good speller. I find interesting words and keep them. I don't like crossword puzzles, though. I'm always looking for a hidden meaning and miss the obvious answer. "It's Hebrew. I think I learned that in social studies."

"Yes, that fits. You're such a smart girl." She drops the book in her lap. "Oh, no."

"What?"

"I don't have a clean blouse for tomorrow. It's in the other suitcase in the car."

"Not to worry. I'll slip on my shoes and run down there and get it." I get up and reach for my shoes.

"I don't want you lugging that heavy case up those stairs. I'll just wear what I had on today."

"Just tell me what you want, and I'll get it out of the case." I start to slip on my shoes.

"Aren't you going to wear socks? It's pretty cool out there." She's frowning at my feet. "Never mind. I don't want to be any trouble."

"It's not any trouble. It'll just take a second." I'm tired, but I didn't mean to raise my voice.

"Well." She hesitates. "If it really wouldn't be too much trouble, just grab the blouse with the blue roses. It's right on top."

"No problem, Lambchop." My shoes are on and I'm out the door.

One street lamp on the other side of the lot dimly lights my path, but I make my way to the car. This place is not nearly as nice as it sounded in the AAA book. Three stars, and not a soul to help us carry our suitcases to the second landing. Just as I reach the car, I nearly jump out of my hide at a sudden shrieking. "Intruder alert! Perimeter warning! Step away from the car," a synthetic voice booms.

"What in the--" I see the Jaguar badge just as the car alarm starts whooping. I step back and see my Buick sitting right beside the British car. I stand there for a few minutes, paralyzed. I don't know whether to worry more about the alarm or what the old man is doing here.

I hear my mother calling my name. She's standing outside our room, her arms wrapped around her to ward off the nippy night air. "It's all right," I call to her. "I accidentally set off somebody's alarm." I point to the lobby. "I'm going to let them know what's going on."

Just then, the old coot steps out of the lobby, followed by the night clerk. He sees me and turns to the clerk. "I must have forgotten to set it properly. Everything's fine." The clerk shrugs and goes back inside.

The old man steps quickly to the car. With a couple of cricket chirps from his remote control, he silences the alarm. Then he turns to me and I say, "See, it's pretty dark, and I thought I was at my car--"

"An understandable mistake. The models are very similar, aren't they?"

"Give or take a few thousand dollars." I don't know why I can't be civil to him.

He looks up and raises a hand in greeting to my mother. “Evening, ma’am.” My mom, mortified to be seen in her nightgown, nods and flees back to the room.

“I’m sorry to have bothered you.” There. I said it. End of discussion, I hope.

“Not at all.” He stands there calmly, looking at me with a steady gaze. I had failed to notice before that his eyes are brown and sparkling. I shouldn’t be able to notice them in this poor light. “Nothing’s an accident. I’ve been hoping for a chance to speak with you privately.”

“Oh?” I should have known -- he’s going to pitch some multi-level marketing scheme.

“You miss your father.” A cold shudder skitters down my spine. My throat tightens. My brain races frantically back to Mom’s lunchtime chatter. No, she didn’t say a word about Dad. “I understand.” He looks at me with -- what? It couldn’t be sorrow. I open my mouth, but no words form. I focus on his face, trying to read his intent. All I can see now is kindness. I feel tears threatening to spill.

He tucks the remote control into his jacket pocket and draws out a little orb of some kind. “I believe you lost this somewhere along the way.” I’m rooted where I stand. “Here.” He steps toward me and extends his hand. A thin blue-white ray from the street lamp illuminates the object. It’s my snowglobe.

This can’t be. While my brain cells dash around in panic, slamming into each other, my body acts for me and reaches for the offering. I cup the globe in my hands. The cold night air seems to recede. The sound of distant traffic fades into silence. Yes, I remember those candy-striped umbrellas and the palm-leafed trees that seemed so exotic to a mountain girl. And I remember the day that Daddy bought it for me. “Daddy, look. Look!” I commanded him, prancing and dancing before the store display.

“What is it, Angel-baby?” He bent down to follow my pointing finger.

“Isn’t it beautiful?” I gasped.

“There’s nothing like a day at the beach,” Daddy agreed. “You want it?” I shook my head up and down so vigorously that my ponytail slapped me in the face.

He was a good man. I continue to stare at the globe. I’m standing very still, yet the particles and liquid begin to swirl. Through the water welling in my eyes, I see golden streaks of sunshine start to twinkle over the scene. And then the light seems to grow. Now the globe is glowing inside and out, white starlight mixing in with the warm radiance. The light stretches and grows. Now it’s reaching for me in the shape of a puppy. I’m looking at nothing but light, but I know this is my little beagle, Randy. The poor fellow was blind and dragging a leg by the time he died. But now he’s a wriggling youngster again. Light licks at my face, and I laugh. I can feel only his love for me.

The light leaps out of my arms and begins to form a circle around me, shutting out the darkness. Someone stands behind me. I turn to face a radiant form. It’s my dad. As tall as ever. He’s still got that tape measure from the store in his hand. Oh, Daddy. My eyes swell with tears. I miss him so much. I need him.

He smiles gently, slides the tape measure in his pocket. Then he moves toward me and squeezes me in his arms. I can smell the menthol of his aftershave. He feels solid. Strong. I lay my head on his shoulder and sob. Great, gulping cries. “Why, Daddy? Why?”

He smoothes my hair and pats my back. I begin to feel calmer. Gently, he releases me from his embrace and stands back. And now I notice just how straight he stands.

Not bent from pain. How he shines with health. With happiness. With freedom. His joy seeps into me. I close my eyes just for a second, relishing this feeling of love and safety. Then, somehow, I know the light is gone. I open my eyes and find the old man smiling at me with gentleness. I feel a little stab of loss, but then I find that I remain encircled by warmth and love.

I struggle to find my voice. "Thank you," comes out as a whisper. "I--I shouldn't ask more of you. Would--" Swallow. "Would you show this to my mother?"

The old man steps closer and reaches for the globe. But instead of taking it from me, his warm hands softly clasp mine, coaxing my fingers to embrace the dome. "This is yours."

He steps back, continuing to smile at me. I search his face, seeking to understand. He says, "I have always been there for your mother." He winks at me. "You're the one I had to chase down." And then the old man raises a hand in farewell, slides into his car and drives off. I peer after the Jag, even after the night envelops it. I hang on to the sound of the purring engine. And then I hear the V-12 roar and I know he's back on the interstate. I stand and stare into the blackness, clutching a little plastic snowglobe to my heart.

Epilogue

Well, I reckon I am finally done. A good thing, because my scissors are dull and I'm too tired to sharpen them. I sewed my way through the bitter winter, daydreaming about redbud trees. From my window, I can see the rose-purple blossoms. Small, new leaves spread over the gray branches of other trees like lace tablecloths, colored just a whisper of the rich green to come.

I did my best with my quilts. I fitted the pieces together in as pleasing a manner as I could. I did a lot more stitching than most folks do these days, not just for looks, but because I want my work to last. I let my spirit flow into every quilt I made. I was fashioned from starlight, and so are my quilts.

Now, what is that racket? I push back from the quilt frame. It takes me a minute to straighten all the way up. Or at least as far as my spine will reach these days. I go to the door and see another car pull up, some green-colored foreign vehicle. Looks like it might be right expensive.

There's a man walking toward me, but I don't see a bag of scraps or any bolts of fabric. I wonder what his business is with me. My eyes have gotten so bad that he's at the door before I can make out his features. Close-cropped hair, whiter than table linen. A face like polished walnut. He's wearing a plain black suit with a snowy white shirt. Oh, I like them fancy-tooled Western boots. That's style.

"Twilight Dawn." His voice is deep and low, and he says my name like it's got magic in it. "I've heard a lot about you. Pleased to finally make your acquaintance."

I examine his face, so I can figure him out. Oh, my. Those dark eyes shine with stars, twinkling and crackling and popping all the way back to the beginning of time.

"Twilight Dawn," he says. "Would you care to take a spin?"

"Yes," I say. "I believe I'm ready."

Notes

Thanks to David Jackson for suggesting the poetry of Edgar Allan Poe, cited extensively in "The Bridge":

Resignedly beneath the sky the melancholy waters lie.
"The City in the Sea," 1831

Herself in the heavens, her beam on the waves. I gazed awhile on her cold smile; too cold -- too cold for me.
"Evening Star," 1827

From childhood's hour I have not been as others were; I have not seen as others saw; I could not bring my passions from a common spring. "Alone," 1830

And, though my faith be broken, and though my heart be broken, here is a ring, as token. "Bridal Ballad," 1837

All that we see or seem is but a dream within a dream.
"A Dream Within a Dream," 1827

I stand amid the roar of a surf-tormented shore.
"A Dream Within a Dream," 1827

They fell: for Heaven to them no hope imparts who hear not for the beating of their hearts. "Al Aaraaf," 1829

"Twilight Dawn" first appeared in *New Millennium Writings*, Summer 2000.

"Junior" first appeared in *Stories*, 1998.

"Full Bloom" won first place in the short story contest sponsored by the Gulf Coast Chapter of the National Writers Association, 2000.

"Picasso's Cat" received honorable mention in the 1999 *Now & Then* Appalachian Fiction Competition.

"The Bridge" won first place for fiction at the 1998 Southwest Florida Writers' Conference.

"Rainbow Ranch" was a finalist in the 1998 Academy Arts Press National Short Fiction Contest.

"Delivery" placed third in the 1998 Westmoreland Art National Poetry and Short Story Competition.

"Reunion" won second prize in the 1997 Academy Arts Press National Short Fiction contest.

"Road Trip" was runner-up in the 1996 short story category of The Soul-Making Literary Prize.